# THE SEARCH

# Liam A. Spinage

# THE SEARCH FOR FAROZAINA

DOUBLE DRAGON

# Chapter 1

We thought the Mare Nostrum was our sea. Every country and city-state with ports and harbours and shores which bordered it claimed a part as its own, as if that great expanse could be owned or tamed. Those who relied on it for trade took it for granted while their counting houses overflowed with coins and goods. Those who claimed to really understand it - from fisherfolk and deckhands to lighthouse keepers and waterwatchers - knew it could never truly be understood and never truly be ours. They knew it exacted a price and watched from the decks and the harbour walls for the day that price would be paid. That day, it turns out, was fast approaching. The startling news washed ashore on every beach where there were ears to hear it and captains from Catapala, the City in the Cliff, last bastion of the old country, to Tepeyac the Gateway in the far west near the Mare Lontana. We were not alone.

Over a period of time several ships had encountered the same alarming spectacle – a great island in the Mare Nostrum, previously uncharted and unheard of even by diviners and scholars as well as those shadowy individuals who make secret knowledge their business. That the island was reportedly spotted in a number of distinct locations caused questions to be raised at the tables of merchants and speculators as to the sobriety of ship captains and caused a flurry of rapid investigation into the reliability of their instruments.

Striking an average of observations taken at separate times - and rejecting the outliers as modern statistical mathematics demanded - you could still assert that this phenomenal island greatly exceeded the dimensions of any uncharted island then known to cartographers of the age, if it existed at all.

Now, it did exist, and since the human mind dotes on objects of wonder, you can understand the tremendous excitement caused by this unearthly apparition. As for relegating it to the realms of fiction, that charge had to be dropped.

It began over the spring equinox, that fortuitous time of the year when the party season begins in earnest for those of us on land, and the winds begin to turn for those at sea. The ship Maliamelita of the Radiant Crown fleet encountered a fog-shrouded island where none had been before, many nautical miles to the southwest out of Lateen harbour. Captain Giaconda Moreno at first thought she was in the presence of an unknown reef and was eager to chart its dimensions so that reports could be filed, and figures updated in the guild ledgers. When the mist momentarily parted to reveal a mountainous island terrain with buildings visible between its three peaks, she called for extra rations of rum and fresh water amongst the crew with the understanding that the root of the hallucination was some seaborne malaise brought on by lack of decent fresh drinking water; a not uncommon occurrence in those times. Further progress toward the island was impeded by a sudden storm and she turned the ship around.

When she reported back and those reports were corroborated by other seafarers along the coast, talk of the island was all the rage throughout every port on the Mare Nostrum. It was sung of in taverns, whispered of in the great churches, and hotly debated in every coffee house. It dominated the front pages of news sheets and made the career of several journalists even as the careers of several skippers were close to ruin as their sanity, sobriety and suitability for duty were brought into question. Mountebanks found in it an opportunity for hatching all sorts of elaborate hoaxes and the cries of their marks echoed across the harbours of Ilforza and Aretina. In those periodicals short of material, there appeared printed speculations of regurgitated mythologies linking the island to some heretofore unmentioned lost civilization and political sabre-rattling suggesting it was clearly some formerly unknown hidden pirate outpost in the midst of the bay.

Neither were our scholarly societies content to sit quietly and watch the show. Endless debates were held, often derailing the rest of the curriculum and always continuing late into the evening. Meanwhile, diviners practised their craft with stars, rivers, entrails, tea leaves and anything else they could contemplate. The 'island question' inflamed all minds. During this memorable campaign, those making a profession of geography and history clashed with those making a profession of wit and satire, spilling waves of abuse, credulity and even drops of blood as the battleground went from the most fanciful of fantasies to the most offensive of personal remarks.

These back-and-forths continued until the end of summer. With inexhaustible zeal, tavern patrons cracked heads over the veracity of the discovery and what it would mean, the most ill-equipped expeditions set forth from Lateen, Perigee, Severa and Faravo into the Mare Nostrum; ships populated only by chancers and sightseers, eager to catch a glimpse of the mysterious mist and its hidden wonders. Sales of spyglasses, sextants and more obscure maritime technology soared to the point where the shop shelves of Lateen were scoured clean. Supposed maps to its location were passed off to unsuspecting shills gathered on the waterfront in an ambitious but unwise race to reach the island and plant their colours upon its fabled shores.

As with other summer sensations, the waves of the phenomenon soon began to break against rockier shores until such time arrived when the storm seemed spent and minds across the known world began to turn back to less fanciful notions. With no further reported sightings, the story of Farozaina might have been short-lived if it were not for the continuing investigations of a number of dedicated individuals and the events that unfolded one autumn morning in Lateen, the City of Sails.

# Chapter 2

I was perfectly placed to witness and recall the tales that were told in quayside tavern and hillside villa alike, and how could I not have been? I had been writing and performing variations on the tale since the news first washed across our southern shores. I had sought out every report and account I could conceive and confabulated them into stirring scripts of comedy, tragedy, morality and horror alike. That summer our performances were praised in every parlour and toasted in every tavern. No one had a greater collection of island tales than I - my racconti dell'isola was a singular work - but I never considered for one moment that there was truth in the smallest one of them. We simply sailed in the wake of the rumours and for a while were the second sensation of that summer. After our theatrics we dined in the most elegant of eateries and were received at the foremost fashionable parties of the season. After several years languishing at the bottom of every playbill, it seemed we had finally found our fortune. Even when innumerable encores tested us to the point of exhaustion, we managed to shine throughout the night as bright as the stars themselves.

A third career sprang up unbidden. In addition to our drama and my divinations, I became sought out as the foremost expert of Farozaina (as I later knew the island to be called by its inhabitants). I confess, I let my newfound fame go to my head. Since so many were keen to have me not hold my tongue, I let it wag. Tall tales fell from my lips as once they had trickled from my quill. After some time though, the subject began to grow wearisome for me and there were several days in high summer when I longed for the peace, if not the poverty, of my former existence as a struggling playwright. My eyes reddened from the many late nights, my senses reeled from the flow of wines and spirituous liquors I was bidden to consume. Finally, my voice itself gave under pressure from all the activity forced upon it and I was made to consign myself to a week away from it all, imbibing such herbal preparations as the finest physics my patrons could afford recommended, until reality became such a blur that I was no more convinced of the existence of Perigee, City of Moons than I was of the mythical Farozaina.

During this period of recuperation, I had a number of well-wishers from within the troupe, but no others. I began to grow anxious that our time in the limelight was done, that our moment had passed. Even though I had hoped in the spring that this time of opportunity and reverie would last forever, I had now resigned myself that our glorious one summer was all that virtue would permit us, and that one singular adventure would suit me just fine. Let the memory of Farozaina fade and with it the memory of the Dusk Till Dawn Theatre.

Then late one night, just as my voice had begun a slow journey to recovery, I was roused from my slumber to find at the door to my lodgings the most unlikely trio of heroes bearing in their arms a singularly unremarkable but large package wrapped up in a plain hessian sack. A fisherman, a soldier and a weather witch – a more comedic threesome has never before walked into a scene. On any other occasion I would have entertained fleeting notions of what events might have brought them into such close keeping with one another. However, since it was my door they were knocking at, and at such an unwholesome hour, it could only mean one thing. They had come seeking my advice about the mysterious island.

My housekeeper let this unlikely company enter and then retired less than tactfully, muttering something about how he didn't get paid to open the door to all-and-sundry in the middle of the night. I made a mental note to remonstrate with him in the morning, though whether for his willingness to leave me alone with three perfect strangers or for his rudeness I did not later recall. As I rekindled the dying hearth for a large pot of coffee, I studied the faces of each of my guests for clues as to who they might be. It was a tactic I had often previously used in crowded taverns to prepare myself for a role; to watch their mannerisms in preparation to mimic them and recreate them later on the stage to the delight of an audience. I could read a history of someone within their eyes, at the corners of their mouth and the way they held their head. It was as sure a technique to me as much as being able to tell their tailor by the cut of their clothes.

The elder man was certainly a seafarer, plain and simple. He wore plain weave breeches and a creased off-white cotton shirt over which was fastened a plain woollen cloak of tan and olive, stained with silt and salt alike. His long hands were tanned and leathery, as was his face. His eyebrows were grey and bushy tapering out to an impressive spread of crow's feet. His eyes spoke of a great tragedy in his distant past brought back to the surface by a recent event, possibly even the one that had brought him here. He shivered occasionally despite the warmth of the room. A single silver ring glinted from a cord around his scrawny neck.

The younger was a more turbulent soul, a soldier for sure, yet one who had not yet quite found his way in life. His eyes darted continuously around the room, taking in his surroundings – impromptu weapons, means of escape. Someone used to continuous alert, he gave the impression that relaxation was something that did not come naturally to him, something he had to force himself to do as a reminder that there were good things in life to be enjoyed if only he took the time for them. He was sturdy and square-footed with a fine set of moustaches and a ring on every finger. His fine clothes had been repatched with loving care several times; sword-cuts, perhaps, or worse. He no doubt had many stories to tell but was only interested in the problem that was immediately occupying him. Not someone you'd want in command, I thought, though he'd made a remarkably effective follower and redoubtable travelling companion.

The young woman stood slightly apart from the men and seemed more aloof – less agitated than the mariner, certainly, who was growing impatient to ask whatever question had delivered them to my abode. She stood with folded arms and refused the offer of coffee, though happily accepted a glass of wine when one was suggested. I surmised she was a latecomer to this party, that the two gentlemen alone had encountered something foreign to them which had led them to seek out her advice before mine. She was more difficult to read than the others, there was a stillness to her eyes and a constant low grin which was a little disquieting. It was only when she stepped forward out of the shadows to accept the wine that I realised there was an unnatural but not unpleasant sheen to her face. Her eyes were wide, and her mouth closed in a wry smile, whereas the men engaged each other constantly in low-level familiar chatter. She wore a ring of gold and pearl on each hand and several bracelets of delicately woven coral and painted shells. I realised then that I recognised the trappings and had in fact spoken to her before – once and very briefly – whilst I was gathering information from sailors and dockworkers about ships that had seen the island: one of the street-magicians who performed weather divinations at the harbour in exchange for a few coins or a swig of wine. Your basic dockside weather watcher? Perhaps, though there were hidden depths there I thought, lurking beneath that unassuming surface. She was dressed much finer now, finer even than the soldier was, but her dress was considerably worn and faded. It looked like she was wearing her one good outfit and, even though it was well taken care of, it had clearly seen better days.

Once the coffee was piping hot and the cream added, I bade the three of them to join me by the fire. By the time the first sip of the dark bitter herbs of my medicine had done their work, I was as keen to hear their tale as they were to tell it. The fisherman spoke first, with frequent enough interjections from the soldier that I discerned a companionship, if not an outright friendship, which had lasted a number of years. Whilst the young woman initially stood, stately and shapely in the shadows, her eyes were continually drawn to the large irregular shaped sack the soldier had carried in over his broad shoulders and deposited gently on the rich red carpet I had recently bought to cover and warm the marble floor. As she stooped over it, I noticed that the dark shapes on the hessian were not caused by some trick of the light or play of the shadows, but by virtue of it being damp. I was perplexed, but did not have to wait long until their story began to play out and I sat on the edge of my chair in wonder, wishing I had deigned to take up the quill the moment they had first entered to record their tale exactly as it was related to me. It will be wise to recount it to you now, as best my memory serves, as within it lie the seeds of our later adventures.

# Chapter 3

In the quiet hour after dawn, Giuseppe adjusted his nets for the third time, waiting for his fishing companion to arrive.

It was unseasonably cold for autumn, even as the mist rolled back across the bay and laid the city of Lateen bare, still wearing its night attire of sultry smoke and dazzling delights. Giuseppe shivered and drew his woollen cloak closer. Dammit, where had Encanto got to? Whilst some of his day-tripper customers often came straight from a night of carousing – despite his warning about the seas getting choppy and upsetting their stomachs – Encanto was usually more sensible. Gruff and occasionally surly, the burly soldier hired the boat for a little quiet time while the mercenary company he belonged to negotiated another contract. He liked to think of it as his little secret; a hobby he was singularly poor at. Trips with Encanto seemed to attract a particularly miserable haul as if the fish themselves took one look at him and swam off laughing. It was worth it to Giuseppe though for the company, the stories and the liquor Encanto usually bought with him, and the inflated price he paid for a day's worth of fishing and company.

Two streets north of the harbour, Encanto broke out into a brief jog, as much to wake himself properly as to make his appointment on time. The early morning air cleared his mind and made him think. Thinking was usually problematic for two reasons – firstly, he was built for action, not thought and secondly there were only two thoughts occupying his mind – where he would be sent next and how much he'd get. His new lover was demanding but craved his coin more than his attention and Encanto's coffers were lacking a little at present.

When he finally caught up with Giuseppe, his boat Ragazzo was ready to sail, rocking impatiently in the waters with the sun peering lazily over the bow as if it was still deciding whether Lateen was ready for it or not. Leaping easily from quay to deck, Encanto landed sure-footedly with a little flourish of his cap to finish. He called over to his companion, who smiled in return. Other fishing boats from other guilds had already sailed away in the hour Giuseppe had been waiting, wondering, shivering in the pre-dawn.

"All set for a good haul?" quipped Encanto breezily, well aware that his luck and lateness both counted against them on that score. Giuseppe bit his lip whilst deciding on the appropriate level of sarcasm for his response. Sure, Encanto presented himself as a bumbling fool and often adopted that character at the masque, but if half what he'd claimed was true he could be a dangerous man to insult.

"The only haul I'll be looking forward to is the one you arrived with!" he riposted, tapping his coin purse and empty wineskin. Giuseppe rubbed his salt-and-pepper beard with his good arm. "Still, we might make a fisherman out of you yet. There, see to the ropes will you and I'll check the sails."

Encanto made swift work of the knots keeping them at rest on the dock and grunted masterfully as he kicked them off away from the harbour wall. The pair of them grinned and set off, the last of the fishing fleet to leave the harbour that fateful autumn morning. If they knew what awaited them that day in the deep waters of the bay, they may have decided to while away the hours in a quayside tavern and count themselves lucky. But fate has a cunning way of catching up with folk even if they're not looking for it and the base fact of the matter is that without that early morning trip things would have turned out vastly different for all of us.

By mid-morning the pair had set all the pots for the day and were busying themselves with Giuseppe's largest net, running it through the pulley and ropes that let them trawl it behind the Ragazzo and haul it in after. At Giuseppe's suggestion, they had deviated from the usual fishing waters, heading further south than they normally would. The winds that favoured them on this journey would likely turn on them later, but since today wasn't actually about fishing – at least in Giuseppe's mind – a later return wouldn't penalise them at the markets later. He had even passed over a few rings to the weather witch Risu, which he often did with day-trippers. It was part of the seafaring experience they were paying for: a few moments watching her throw a handful of old fish bones on the quayside, run her fingers through some seaweed and kiss the wind good luck for them. Many of them even bought some of her shell trinkets. Giuseppe had noticed that despite the cheap theatrics, Risu was rarely if ever wrong about the weather. If a storm was coming in, she knew before the dark clouds began to gather. For a superstitious mariner, she was a blessing. Encanto disagreed and had stood behind him, guffawing occasionally into his kerchief and stifling deeper laughter with his sleeve. Risu, for her part, occasionally rolled her eyes at Encanto but was otherwise the consummate professional. This was what the pair were currently arguing about on the boat – whether Risu believed her own predictions or whether she was merely acting a role. Even Encanto had to believe it was a surprisingly good act for a dockside seareader.

After the third trawl they had managed to net just one single fish, which looked so lonely, lost and laughable that they threw it back and decided to have an early luncheon. Sitting on barrels on the deck of the Ragazzo, they passed Encanto's wineskin back and forth until it was nearly empty and enjoyed a simple meal of flatbreads, a tangy, crumbly white cheese and a thick, sweet sauce Encanto claimed was 'all the rage' in well-to-do Perigee, to which Giuseppe muttered a response about palates being too refined these days to enjoy the simpler pleasures of crabs and clam chowder. In between mouthfuls, Encanto regaled his companion with tales of daring adventure in the streets of Severa and the tombs of Vilarica, whilst Giuseppe pointed out the larger sea life in the distance. In short, they became so merry that they were unaware then just how far south the winds and currents had taken them.

Both of them later assured me that despite its prevalence in tavern talk at the time, neither of them mentioned Farozaina on this trip. It appears that by this stage they both considered it to be a myth and their conversations about it had already played out, their discourse dissipated in the waves lapping against the bow of the boat.

# Chapter 4

Whilst Encanto was enjoying a day of leisure, his brother Matthias was being summoned. Whilst he displayed open loyalty to his company, Sarabande, his situation with regards to the Balance of Twilight guild was a little more complicated.

The Balance of Twilight happened to be the most prestigious intelligencer guild in the city at that time, perhaps in the whole of Ilforza. I myself had encountered their agents that summer and had been impressed by their display of generosity toward the Dusk Till Dawn theatre troupe. That was before I knew that it was me that they really wanted, or rather the knowledge I had gathered on Farozaina. It seems I had done a better job in this regard than several of their members who they had set on the task. Agents both overt and covert had been dispatched by this guild to 'get to the truth of the island matter'. For the guild interests, I understood from my then-limited perspective, were best served by maintenance of the status quo and the normal flow of information which was their stock-in-trade was being replaced with a steady flow of rumours and speculation about the island. If the island was the only topic of conversation, as indeed it was that summer, then the regular society gossip and balance of allegiances were shifting beneath the surface. The pool of information had been polluted. That was how they spun it to me, and I had little reason to disbelieve them at the time, though in retrospect I should have been more circumspect.

The reasons I had not been were threefold. One: I knew they could make or break my career if they so chose. Two: I was overwhelmed by the magnificence of the palatial estate I had been called to. Three: I was one of those responsible for that pollution, feeding the flames of fantasy with my quill and my troupe and whilst I felt no guilt at this – my very profession relies on such, after all - they could have taken a very different course with me to get to the information I had. Instead, they wined, dined and flattered me until I eventually told them everything I knew and thought no harm of it. I would later reflect on that folly, of course, when I found myself imprisoned; but here I get ahead of myself, reader! We shall return to the matter of Matthias and the reason he had been called forward.

Matthias was as different to his brother as was possible for two siblings to be without speculation arising as to any common ancestry. He was taller and leaner than Encanto and took much more care over his appearance. In manner, he was professional and aloof where Encanto was gruff but avuncular. These differences led the brothers in two different directions; though they loosely shared the same profession, the clients they attracted and the mercenary companies who hired them meant they had disparate lifestyles and little in common in those days.

"You are correct. A champion is what we seek." Matthias shifted a little, somewhat uncomfortably, and peered through the gloom at the one addressing him. There are few who have looked on the true face of Chiaroscuro, head of the Balance of Twilight. In a business where knowledge is power, she preferred to remain functionally invisible. To that end, she always wore a mask, half white and half black though which colour was on the left or right changed from account to account from those who had met with her. Those invited to her presence were blindfolded for the journey so that they knew not their destination. Her greeting room was a masterpiece of architecture, with slowly burning braziers set in bas-relief in the walls in between reflective surfaces so that one was never quite sure where to look. If there was any profession that was more smoke-and-mirrors than mine, this was it and Chiaroscuro sat at the heart of it. For Matthias to be called here and offered the role as guild champion was the pinnacle of his career and should have been the destination of a long and dangerous adventure, a sign of his arrival in the halls of power. He knew as much but was yet reticent, an element of trust somehow holding him back. He hadn't gotten this far and still lived without a finely honed survival instinct and at the moment it was setting off every alarm conceivable. "Still," he thought, "It would be better to agree now and work out any troubles later." For all he knew, refusal at this point might even be more dangerous.

A deal was therefore struck, a contract signed. Everyone would know his new loyalty and doors which once were closed would now open. He was introduced to new fish in a bigger pond and played the part of the minnow. What intrigued and disturbed him the most, he mused – even as a seamstress adjusted his newly purchased doublet while he stared in the mirror – was that the guild asked so little of him. He was certain they were preparing him for something to come but told him nothing other than to be ready. They insisted that he not take on any other work which might take him out of the city but paid him well enough that he did not feel the need for such anyway.

In short, he was bored. He spent his days on a routine of training, exercise and study in his guild-appointed room at the Sybella but did little else. Instead, he waited, watching and coiled like a spring, until the Balance of Twilight sought fit to complete the tableau they had arranged him in.

# Chapter 5

A sharp tug on the Ragazzo's windlass raised Encanto from his reverie and gave Giuseppe a good scare. The pair jumped up instantly, scattering crumbs of cheese across the deck for the mice to fight over later. They rushed as one to the stern to see what manner of catch was large enough for them to feel the tug from their deck chairs. Larger fish were rare in these waters – rarer still with Encanto's singular reputation – and they were both interested. What their initial feelings were when they saw what was in the net, they would later disagree on in their accounts to me, but it was clear from their initial assessment that they were out of their depth, so to speak.

Tangled in the net was a creature the likes of which neither of them had ever caught sight of. Encanto first thought he saw a woman. Giuseppe swore he saw a large fish with a mass of kelp. Only when she shifted and struggled to escape did they both realise that it was the same thing. A mermaid.

Stories of merfolk are of course common in every port of the Mare Nostrum, from Tepeyac the Gateway in the far-off west to Jiya, the City of Dreams on the southern shore. Certainly, though, none had ever been caught in a fishing net. This was something new entirely, a person to be rescued, an adventure to be had, a tale to tell at the quayside in exchange for a round of drinks. It would of course prove to be so much more in due course; but as for now our two unlikely heroes tried their best to deal with the situation as best they could.

After only a short time, it became obvious that the mermaid was tearing at the net in order to free herself, both with her arms and a fine set of very sharp teeth with which she was trying to bite through the mesh. She was thrashing around so violently that her frantic efforts were having very little effect, but in order for them to free her from their net they would have to drag it aboard and cut it open, by no means an easy feat with a struggling, scared figure within. Encanto braced himself for the haul and Giuseppe winced as the winch creaked and groaned as Encanto strained to turn the handle. The mermaid ceased struggling, and the pair thought perhaps she realised that her release and safety were in their hands. As they brought her on deck, however, they realised that she had ceased breathing and began to flop around on the deck still entangled much like the first fish they had caught and thrown back.

Encanto rushed over for a bucket of water and immediately poured it over her head with a flourish of triumph. Giuseppe looked up at him with a sarcastic shrug from where he was busy cutting through the mesh with his gutting knife. "Put her head in the water, fool, not the other way round!" Encanto spun on his heels and raced off for the second fire bucket, Giuseppe was just over halfway through the netting. Their unexpected guest was beginning to give up the ghost, which thankfully made both of their jobs easier but also made them both work with more haste than speed. Encanto nearly tripped on a rope on his return, by which time Giuseppe had finally cut a clear passage through the net and had moved the remainder of it out of the way. Encanto grabbed the mermaid's limp head and held it down in the water bucket, just as his brother had done to him countless times when trying to sober him up.

By the time they had gotten this far, both of them were exhausted from their sudden flurry of recent activity. Their guest was alive but constrained to breathing from a limited water supply and was obviously far from comfortable. (She was later to tell us just how close she had in fact come to dying, as well as how infuriated she had been at the pair of them at the time).

Now the immediate problem had been resolved, at least temporarily, they had to decide what to do next. Of course, they could have merely decided to return her to the sea at that point and be done with it. Sometimes I wish they had. Encanto had begun thinking what would happen if they took her back to Lateen. It wasn't clear that she could think or talk at all, was she a mere animal of sorts albeit one with a partially human appearance? He didn't know, and no amount of scratching his head and wringing his hands would help him. He later admitted that he thought for all of two seconds that 'she would have made a fine prize and fetched a good price', but not within her earshot and seemed wholly embarrassed that he had entertained such a notion at all. Giuseppe wanted to take her to Risu, at which Encanto raised an eyebrow of surprise. The mariner simply stared back and won the argument by simply being the only one with a solid plan at all. He pointed out that the mermaid appeared to be injured – there were a series of scratches and what could easily be a knife wound on her midriff. He tried to clean the wound but then realised that he had no idea at all what he was doing – maybe saltwater was the best thing for a mermaid's wound? At this point she raised her head from the bucket, screamed something which sounded like "Kweee-arrk" and passed out again.

# Chapter 6

Preparations were made and a course was set. Unsure of what they had encountered or where it would take them, Encanto and Giuseppe had opted to seek the counsel of Risu, who in addition to her reputed divinatory powers also had some of the skills of the physic. Giuseppe was a little troubled at how far south they had travelled and how late they would return; Encanto took to fretting over the young girl whose pallor was still unrelentingly pale green, her skin cold, her heartbeat irregular.

She could, from the waist up, have been mistaken for a young lass of maybe eleven or twelve, but for the sea-green hue of her skin. She wore some garments fashioned from the weeds of the sea which evidently allowed her maximum freedom of movement underwater whilst still giving the appearance of being stylish: a tapered blouse whose arms finished in elaborate puffed cuffs just below the elbow and a series of buttons down the front which, on closer inspection, turned out to be the most exquisite silvery pearls. Each of these might fetch twenty ducats or more as a treasure alone, the entire garment in good repair would exceed the sum of the pearls by a likewise amount. One had broken off and one of the sleeves was slashed a little at the shoulder – not in the popular Lateen fashion but rather by an instrument of violence as a gash of blood beneath testified. This seemed to be the deepest wound on her body. There were several small scratches marring the otherwise serene contours of her face and a swelling at the rear of her scalp, beneath a blood-matted clump of her plaited cerulean hair.

Beneath the waist there could be no human comparison made at all – a long tail of scales, free now from the netting that had concealed it earlier. Here were scales as silvery bright as the undulating ocean on any moonlit night, shot through with streaks of blues and purples so deep in hue that one might be forgiven at first glimpse for mistaking them as black. They were in point of fact - as the astrologer Paratiritis was later to remark - nuances on the purity of colours in the night sky whilst the glistening pinpoints of white-gold could represent a constellation above. I never did see the comparison fully (though I never confessed as much, fearing as I did that he might raise his eyebrows, take in breath and launch at me again with such rapidity of speech that the force of the words made me retreat across the deck).

Whilst Encanto took care to make sure the maid was watched over sufficiently that she might survive the journey back to the coast (and pocketed one of those pearl buttons), Giuseppe made good with the rope, tack and the sails. The winds seemed to favour them, and they were back at harbour not long after night had spread its feast of stars over the bay. None were surprised when the fishing boat was the last to return, less still that it returned again with nets empty. Giuseppe could pay his guild dues with what he had earned from Encanto and supplement it by telling the tale of the day they caught a mermaid.

When they reached the harbour wall, Risu was sitting there waiting for them, bare feet dangling in the water lapping against the smooth stones at high tide, her face creased and wrinkled but with a moon-lit countenance which made her skin shimmer and her smile beatific.

"I believe, gentlemen, that you may need my services."

# Chapter 7

Encanto at once wondered how it was that Risu knew to be there waiting for them, but Giuseppe held him back with a whisper. "She's a diviner, remember?" Encanto raised a sceptical eyebrow but agreed they couldn't afford to interrogate and antagonise the one person who they thought could help.

Risu stood and folded her arms impatiently, waiting for the two men to tie up the boat. If either of them had shot a glance her way, they may have noticed a smug grin spread across her face. When Encanto did finally look up, it was with a remonstration. "You could give us a hand here! Look, this is what we wanted to talk to you about. She needs proper help." He emphasised 'proper' with the indication that that was exactly the sort of help she couldn't give. He'd seen a variety of street charlatans in his time and fallen prone to more than one in his youth and wasn't about to give her dubious talents any credit until he'd actually seen them in action.

Risu looked down at the mermaid and paled visibly. She beckoned Encanto to pass her up gently and lay her on the dockside so that she could inspect her wounds. Giuseppe, having secured the last mainstay, came to his assistance. The three of them stood on the quayside in silence in the chilly night air, peering down at the unexpected catch of the day. Risu fumbled with one of the many pouches at her belt; Encanto half-expected her to produce some animal bones to wave over her whilst she performed some dubious divination. Instead, she produced a small phial which she hurried uncorked and waved underneath the mermaid's nose. Instantly the girl began to inhale deeply, cough and then sneeze violently. What sounded like a lengthy list of expletives - judging from her facial expressions - shot from her open mouth. Then she fell silent again when she gazed up at Risu's quizzical, concerned expression.

"She's safe to move, for now. I suggest we retire to my hut nearby. We need to make plans."

Encanto was about to retort but thought the better of it. He picked the girl up gently in his arms and resigned himself to the hope that soon all their questions would be answered. Giuseppe took a last glance back at the Ragazzo to make sure it was properly tied and followed in his wake. Risu trailed behind them, her heart racing even at the slow pace they were making. As they rounded the dockyard from wooden jetty to cobbled quay, she looked out over the gently waving ocean.

"I don't understand. It wasn't supposed to happen like this, it never happens like this." If I had been present to interpret that statement or those looks, I might have noticed then a veneer of concern and trepidation masking genuine fear in her heart. That might have given me an idea of what we were to expect.

The interior of Risu's shack was well appointed, but small and crude by Lateen standards and ridiculously cluttered. Encanto felt like he was about to trip over something everywhere he went or accidentally knock over a stack of books and send them sprawling noisily across the floor. Threadbare carpets and rugs hugged every inch of floorspace, various unruly house plants competed for light and their leaves and fronds thrust out at every conceivable level from ankle to shoulder. Encanto had a hard time negotiating passage through to where he could safely and gingerly deposit their passenger - a long, faded green divan which looked to be the only furniture in the room that wasn't covered with maps, nautical charts, or various boxed curios of skeletal fish parts. He seemed genuinely worried he might have made the patient's injuries worse.

Giuseppe emerged from behind a series of green drapes which Encanto realised was actually seaweed, carrying a tray of chipped cups. He'd clearly been here before and not for the first time Encanto became annoyed at the unspoken history between the two.

Risu immediately went over to her unconscious guest and bent over her with concern, stroked her hair with tenderness and spoke close to her ear in soft, soothing tones. "Don't worry, little one. We will make sure you are well again."

"You don't seem at all concerned at seeing your first mermaid." Encanto's impatience got the better of him. "And just how did you know that you might be needed, hmm?" He waved his finger at Risu in a gesture of accusation, but she appeared not to pick up on the movement or the tone in his voice. Finally, ignored for the last time, he sat down on a tiny stool that was far too small for him and accepted a cup of clove-spiced rum from Giuseppe which he then sipped at sulkily whilst stealing glances across at the divan.

Risu had begun to dress the wounds with some nasty-smelling poultices which clogged up the already dust-thick air with a heady, fishy aroma that only a sailor could love. The patient responded well at first though her voice was still weak. When she first opened her eyes, she panicked immediately upon seeing her surroundings and the looming figure of Risu in the dimly lit room, her eyes wide open in horror. Risu was forced to sedate her in order to ensure she did not injure herself further and managed a brief, whispered conversation before the maid fell into a deep torpor. Seemingly satisfied there was no more that could be done, Risu turned to Giuseppe and Encanto, finally ready to tell them what she knew.

"This is not my first encounter with a mermaid." She had the good grace to pause momentarily and allow Encanto a brief gloating glare. "There are...tales among diviners in general and seareaders in particular. I have not met one before except within the covers of a book" - she pointed now back at a stacked shelf over her left shoulder which was partially hidden by ferns - "but I have divined the truth of those tomes. Never did I imagine I might see one. They are alleged to live in a city beneath the sea, hidden from the sight of all others. This young lady we have here is no less than the daughter of the king himself. I know this from the tales in those books and by the name she surrendered to me before she fell back into rest - Lacrimanta."

She paused for effect, but the effect was naught more than a stunned silence. Encanto lost the remainder of his doubt at her artifice, Giuseppe looked hurt more than anything, sorry perhaps that there was more to Risu than he believed, as if a great wave had crashed his consciousness and left his mind in salty foam.

"The city itself has never been seen by outsiders. Recently, though, the island which floats above it has been viewed by many mariners. The tavern tales are true. Farozaina waits out there, somewhere in the great expanse of the Mare Nostrum, or perhaps even the Mare Lontana beyond. We have with us what may be its greatest prize, the king's own dear daughter. If we were to return her to her father, it would be a kindness to be repaid with a king's ransom - riches and knowledge beyond our wildest dreams. This I know. This is what the lore reveals and what I have heard from the lips of my own father. What I do not know is where to find the island or the city. Should we be able to accomplish that, enough fame and fortune await us that we may sit the rest of our lives comfortably on a palatial estate, should we so wish. The question is, are we prepared to undertake such a venture? And more so, do we know of any who might assist us in locating the island and securing our place in the books of history?" Her tale over, she sat down somewhat wearily, but with an impish expression on her brow and a sparkle in her eyes that suggested a willingness to join in any escapade, to live through one of the myths and gaze upon the glory of Farozaina.

Both men responded positively and instantly. To the first question they had only to agree with an emphatic 'Aye'. As to the second question, only one name came to their lips: mine.

# Chapter 8

When the fisherman, the soldier and the diviner had at last finished their tale, the coffee pot had twice been exhausted of contents and Risu had made her way through half a bottle of Pride of Socotra 142 (considered one of the better years due to the scarcity of the grape following a harsh winter rather than any noticeable improvement in flavour). Two plates of pastries had also been consumed, the remaining crumbs of which were balanced precariously on Encanto's drooping moustaches, though the fine fellow seemed oblivious to their predicament. All thoughts were on the young Lacrimanta, curled up and asleep now in the marble bath in the next room. No doubt that would be a surprise to my housekeeper when he awoke to prepare the breakfast. That time could not be far off now, as the first fingers of dawn began to pry their way through the balcony shutters (It was, and possibly still is, considered unfashionable to have an east-facing apartment in Lateen due to the time one is then forced to greet the inevitability of the dawn. The major consequence of this was that such dwellings were available for a fraction of the price. I was famous, not rich). We therefore had a series of decisions to make in quick succession. Who else could or should we tell? Where might Lacrimanta stay and remain hidden while she recovered her health enough to communicate and express her wishes? And of course, the inevitable 'what then?' which underwrote every decision. Unless I was willing to add my gossipy housekeeper to our little ring of secret-keepers, it was clear that some immediate subterfuge was in order to put him off the scent, or we would have to move the girl again before the city began to yawn, stretch and open their blinds to permit the proud procession of the morning sun.

Further to our nocturnal narration, I myself had yet to give an accurate account of my accumulated understanding on the subject - which was, after all, what the trio had aroused me to procure. Immediate arrangements needed to be undertaken first though. We were initially at quite a loss as to how to proceed until I recalled that there was one in my troupe whose sister owned a bathhouse we often frequented in leisure and moreover it was currently closed for the winter (the sea being wholly inadequate for social bathing throughout the year, but indoor bathing being practised solely as a summer evening activity. Maritime engineering was strong in Lateen, heating engineering somewhat lacking). I endeavoured therefore to impress on my guests that we should try and make Lacrimanta comfortable there for it was clear to all that she would prefer an aquatic environment in which to recuperate. The establishment in question was some six streets hence; we therefore made haste there and arrived none too soon. I made use of the skills of my misspent youth to part the door from its beloved lock, reminding myself to send a messenger as soon as possible to beg forgiveness from my fellow thespian and his relative. Within a few further moments we had gently laid Lacrimanta in the pool and whilst she would rather have prepared saltwater to fresh, she nevertheless began to swim- awkwardly and favouring her left side - but contentedly. (She was later to insist we added salt to the water to make her more comfortable. This was one of the many demands she made upon our time and patience which we tried to bear with good grace given the situation. She was, after all, a princess of her people and was accustomed to being accommodated).

This task accomplished, we took advantage of the early hours to break our fast uninterrupted by others in a delightful, secluded cafe which - having made the interesting decision only to serve mint tea and fruit in the Amouion style rather than the bitter coffee and rich sugary pastries which were the fashionable Lateen breakfast at the time - enjoyed a level of relaxed solitude even at the busiest hour of the morning and was completely empty when we arrived. The proprietor, who I had made nodding acquaintance with during the stay in my new premises (when I write, I usually do so without my residence since the possibilities for distractions whilst at home prove too much for my addled brain), nodded me over to the best table and seemed pleased that I had company, though perplexed at our early hour. Once we had settled and begun sipping from our steaming glasses, I began to elucidate on the subject of the island whilst pausing occasionally to enjoy the thin slices of apricot, peach and melon on the plate before me. I enjoyed the captivity of the audience, naturally, and warmed to the telling of the tale, starting with my first idea to satirise the island mania gripping the docks and finishing with my current predicament and illness. I named everyone I could recall speaking to, listed every map and document I had researched, and tried to separate the fact from the fiction. I suggested that given we now knew certain facts from the folk-tales passed to Risu, we were in a prime position to look for the island, though such an undertaking would be costly - beyond the combination of wealth the four of us had amassed in our lives - and undoubtedly draw some attention. Four more city folk heading into the sea on a misguided journey to find the island would be written off as a joke. The four of us doing the same would undoubtedly raise certain eyebrows in the information industry rife among the intelligencer guilds, even before we managed to obtain and outfit a ship and crew and then sneak aboard that craft our bathhouse mermaid princess.

I was well connected enough to have several patrons, though, who might be willing to offer me funds for a new play. With a little subterfuge, a sea voyage could be seen as an excellent gimmick to advertise a new island story (I had yet to give it the full operatic treatment, though I had several arias composed and ready to rehearse). I suggested a prime opportunity to do this would be at the Bounty of the Sea Ball in a week's time. Though this festive annual event was one of the tackier spectacles in the Lateen calendar, it was seized on with relish by many as either the last ball of autumn or the first of winter, depending on who was being asked. I had naturally been invited myself - we were due to perform at it owing to our troupe's current reputation - and was sure to be able to bring in three additional stagehands.

My new companions found this eminently agreeable and were excited that I had given them the answers they sought and a direction in which to proceed. We resolved to meet again at the bathhouse several times during the week so that Lacrimanta would not be unaccompanied or bored and to begin plans for both the ball and, beyond that, for our excursion into the great blue yonder. We then retired to our separate houses, the night's adventures having caught up with each of us and slept soundly dreaming of riches beneath the sea and beyond our imagination.

# Chapter 9

"Everything is in readiness?"

Even though it was phrased as one, it was not really a question, not when it came from the mouth of the king. Mauvid knew better than that – she had served as the captain of the guard for twenty long years and had never known his Hadal Majesty to ask a question the answer to which he did not already know. The questions were more a convenient way to explore the current state of knowledge of the addressee, their willingness to divulge and how they choose to respond. Mauvid merely nodded, as was her custom. The king naturally understood her response perfectly, their relationship refined over a matter of years to the point where she began to wonder why the king had articulated the question in the first instance, rather than merely shooting her a glance.

Her second, a recent addition to the barrack, was more verbose in reply, which settled that answer in Mauvid's mind. "The island has been spotted by several seafarers in the waters above, your Hadal Majesty. Our agents among the dirt-dwellers, compounded with our own significant proficiency in the divinatory arts, suggest that events should reach their peak, shortly plateau, then escalate again in just over two moons. The tides are right." With this response came an accompanying bow, swift and deep enough to cause a turbulence in the waters around them, so that a school of nearby starburst jellyfish darted away from the coral throne as if the king himself had commanded them forth on a mission of the utmost urgency.

"The tides are right'. The king responded in kind, then waved a dismissal to the young soldier and his commander. They swam out of the cave and downward toward the barrack, the entire of Hadala, City Under the Sea spread beneath them - from the depths of the Chasm of Sorrows to the heights of the Spires of Joy. Dim, pure-white lights gleamed from the many homes carved into the submarine cliff faces and across the bed itself. Above them - far above them - lay the island of Farozaina.

# Chapter 10

If it is true that the ambition of a hostess can be measured by the complexity of their hairstyle, then Julietta Sancorvo was very ambitious indeed. Her braids were thrice-curled and ran in fine spirals to their gold-tipped apexes. From humble beginnings in Navis through an apprenticeship and a career as a maker of masquerade costumes, she had risen to become the premier hostess in all Lateen, leaving a stream of eager admirers and heartbroken fools alike in the wake of her emerald green ballgown.

As hostess and organiser of the Bounty of the Sea ball, she was already having a stressful day. Three servants had to be dismissed for incompetence, two more for spying. The scaffolding on the replica ships deck and rigging she'd had built in her ballroom needed stabilising, the first batch of desserts hadn't set correctly and had to be thrown out. She tried to ride this out with good humour, but her patience was sorely tested.

At least the theatre troupe was already in place and rehearsing. Julietta glanced over. Two of the performers were just sitting on side chairs watching the others and pointing. *Well, that was their problem.* At least they looked the part, although why they were already in costume was beyond her. She had plenty of other arrangements to occupy her time though - the blue and white 'sea foam' carpets were due to arrive any moment and she'd have to summon more staff to lay them out according to her designs. With an exhalation of breath somewhere between a huff and a sigh, she strode out of the entrance hall, trailing three seamstresses, a hairdresser and a sous-chef all demanding her immediate attention.

Giuseppe and Encanto watched her go from their chairs, oblivious as to who she was. They had tried helping set the stage, but I had quickly grown weary of Encanto's amateurish buffoonery and told them to wait out of the way. Giuseppe had tied some fine ropes but that was the limit of his skill. Neither of them seemed inclined to any artistic leanings. Risu was different; she padded across the stage altering the position of several key props and adding small items to the display. This first annoyed me - I had been very specific in my direction - until I saw the desired result from the auditorium. When lit this evening, the shadows of each would be cast in a particular way on the backdrop itself so as to give the impression of great sea beasts swimming on and under the ocean. She smiled in her odd way, as pleased with the result as I was but showing it less.

"Shadow play," she smiled. "As effective as smoke and mirrors, in its way. Everyone will see something a little different depending on where they are in relation to the lights, which will add to the chatter when they talk about the play later at the ball."

I nodded in superlative agreement. The stage was set - figuratively and literally - for the masquerade later in the evening where we would woo each of my four patrons to the idea of backing an island opera, based on a dangerous sea voyage to a mythical place which we ourselves would undertake as prelude and marketing exercise alike.

\*\*\*

When the evening finally came, Julietta's mansion had been utterly transformed with reams of blue silk damask. Waiting staff clad in midnight blue livery served chilled wines and cool water, their silver trays holding small bowls of iced caviar and seashells of spun sugar. While Giuseppe and Encanto waited backstage, Risu and I mingled with the guests, and I pointed out each principal patron as they approached. She herself wore a fine gown of ultramarine with puffed aquamarine sleeves - which she admitted to having borrowed from the hostess - and a fine double set of pearls which she insisted were a family heirloom.

"Who are our options for patronage, then?" Risu whispered to me as the guests began to arrive. "Besides our short-tempered hostess, of course." She dipped a breadstick into a scallop full of taramasalata and twirled it playfully.

I turned, temporarily astounded but admiring her powers of observation more at every passing moment.

"Oh, come - she has more money than sense, little patience for her staff or guests, yet insists on hosting this ball every year? She has to be a player."

I agreed readily, then pointed a finger to where an elderly, bearded gentleman in a red and gold brocade doublet was in hushed conversation with a young redhead in a swan feather mask to accentuate her angular, bird-like features. "There are our two prime factors: Nonavetti, who they call the

46

heartbreaker for all the young men and women whose lives are shattered by her presence and old Buolio who won his shipbuilding business in a game of chance and has wandered lazily through his life without lifting a finger. The fourth patron I wouldn't recognise without their trademark mask - Chiaroscuro of the..."

"There she is!" noted Risu, nudging me slightly so that my turn did not look forced. Surrounded by bodyguards, even at a ball. What kind of life is that?"

"A respectable and well-rewarded one. You've met her before, then?"

Risu, for whatever reason, chose not to answer, instead asking me a further question. "How should we make our approaches? Directly or obliquely, do you think?"

"You didn't read the script, then? I wrote it especially for this evening's entertainment! The play's the thing. There are four sisters who are in fact rivers: each of them finds its way to the sea, but it's only the water of the four of them combined that raises the ship enough to clear the harbour. I've laid it on thick. With any luck, they will fall over themselves trying to offer more money than each other."

It was Risu's turn to look astonished and admired. "I never knew," she said, prodding me with a breadstick, "that you had such hidden depths."

I blushed. "I'm certainly not as shallow as I look!"

Before we could say more, a servant approached us and told us that the play was shortly to begin.

# Chapter 11

"A veritable masterpiece of theatre!" Buolio was the first of our prospective patrons to approach and did not stint on his praise. It was our fervent hope he would not stint on his generosity either.

Our hostess Julietta also joined us: behind her an army of silver-salvered servants rushed forward to offer us every viand available from seaweed and crab vol-au-vents to candied starfish. We also each took a glass of the excellent wine - a sweet Albarino with an intense citrus taste and heady floral notes.

"You know," Buolio leaned in and confessed in a confidential whisper, "I wonder if we could have a quiet word? I would love to get in on a production on the, ah, ground floor so to speak."

"I doubt you're the only one." Julietta flicked her head back toward Nonavetti who was circling our little group, idly toying with her glass.

"What? Oh, I, er…well…"

Julietta sighed and smiled. "Buolio, darling, I would be surprised if the whole room hadn't heard you. Really, with a voice so clear and strong I wonder if you should not be on the stage yourself!"

Buolio's white face became as red as a Safira sunset, and he stuttered. "Well, good of you to say so, Julietta." He puffed out his chest and cleared his throat. Nonavetti took this moment to introduce herself to us.

"I couldn't help overhearing…the delight of a new performance from Dusk Till Dawn! What delicious folly!" She turned to Buolio, who flushed again. "I have been on the stage myself of course. Do you think there could be a part in your production for me?" This last line was delivered to myself, eye to eye. It took an elbow in the back from Risu to break her gaze.

"Well, naturally, I..."

"Let us take our business somewhere more discreet, no? There's no reason to offer speculation on our conversation to all and sundry. Please, follow me." Julietta turned and led us away to a section of wall wherein was inlaid a door handle cleverly disguised as a decorative motif of a reclining nude.

"Enter, if you will." She paused only to collect an envelope which had been proffered to her by a messenger. Upon picking it up, she placed it into my hand. "For you, I believe."

I looked down at my name for a moment, wondering who it was from and what etiquette I might breach by opening it immediately.

"I can provide a ship for the voyage, that goes without saying..." Buolio was in full flow now, talking excitedly to Risu who smiled at his every word.

"Provisioning shouldn't be a problem. I can name several outfitters who would jump at the chance." Julietta interjected, tired of what would likely become a rambling Buolio monologue.

"People seem to like lavishing me with gifts." Nonavetti was keen not to be outdone. "I see no reason not to share that generosity with you. Now, about that role I had in mind. Is there a mermaid in your play?"

I nearly choked on my wine. Risu looked over at me nervously, gave me a single glance and then spoke up.

"Oh, what a wonderful idea! You would be a perfect mermaid, Nonavetti!"

The young lady beamed at her suggestion. I was still dumbstruck - luckily Risu had been able to seize on the opportunity.

"Well, that's me sold then. To fame!" Her swan mask brushed against my own as she clinked her glass to mine.

"I'm in." Buolio sensed an opportunity, too. "To fortune!"

"I'll have some papers drawn up." Julietta seemed no less keen than the others but was understandably more circumspect in her dealings. "To success!"

So that only left...I looked down cautiously at the envelope unopened in my lap. Perhaps....?

"To adventure!" Risu clinked glasses with everyone. "May we all find what we seek in this courageous endeavour. Now, if you will excuse us, I believe we need a moment in private to discuss those offers before us."

"Certainly. I should not neglect my other guests! Let us meet again soon to go over the details." Julietta stood and bade the others follow her back into the ballroom, leaving the two of us quite alone.

When they were gone and the door closed behind them, I finally turned to Risu and voiced my concern. "How do you imagine she got to learn of our aquatic princess? Or do you perhaps believe it was purely a coincidence?"

"Perhaps merely a lucky guess, but I suspect not. I sense another hand at work. Who is the letter from?"

I opened it cautiously with an apple knife which had been discarded on a nearby dresser.

"Ah."

Risu moved beside me and looked over my shoulder.

*Let the others believe what they will.*

*You have the full support of my guild's resources in your true venture.*

The missive was unsigned, but a second glance at the seal on the envelope answered our question: two masks - one white, one black - intertwined with a mirror service as backdrop.

"Four for four." Risu downed the remainder of her wine. "Well played."

# Chapter 12

Matthias looked down at the two envelopes in his hand. The first was to be delivered to a guest at the ball - the writer of the play they had all just enjoyed. The second was addressed to him and contained his instructions for later. Finally, something to exercise his many talents.

He palmed the first off on a nearby waiter, confident that would be sufficient to ensure its delivery. Such routine messengering was beneath his role as champion. He was about to open the second when a familiar shadow loomed over him.

"Enjoying the new work?" His brother stood beside him, full glass in hand, his tone sarcastic.

Matthias returned his gaze disdainfully. "Go away, little brother. I'm on official business, I can't have you showing me up. What are you even doing here anyway?" That was an afterthought, which in retrospect he probably shouldn't have voiced out loud. Dammit, but his bungling brother could bring out the temper in him, even now. He made efforts to stand back to attention, his eyes circling the room, fervently wishing Encanto would embarrass him no further but resigned to the fact he was asking the impossible.

"I'm on business too," Encanto replied. He touched the side of his nose with his finger in a gesture of emphasis. "Secret business. Way more important than bodyguarding. You wouldn't understand." He was enjoying this moment immensely.

Matthias swung round, too quick for Encanto to avoid the swift punch to his gut. With a quick glance around to make sure they hadn't attracted too much attention, he helped Encanto up and half-carried him to a side room where they could argue in peace.

"I warned you once. What do you want? Why can't you just let me enjoy what I've worked so hard to achieve?"

Encanto, suitably recovered now, made a quick attempt to punch Matthias back, but was too slow - the blow glanced off his hauberk and grazed his knuckle. Then he sat down, all the fight taken out of him, glum as a Murmur Monday.

"Look, I might be able to get you some work out of this. Let me have a talk with the new boss, I'm sure I can fix you up with something."

"I don't need your hand-me-down contracts!" Encanto responded in an angry sulk. "I'm on the cusp of something big, brother, bigger than you'll know. Yes, it may have just been dumb luck, but it's my dumb luck, dammit!" He pulled himself to his feet. "Now, if you don't mind, I have work to do."

Matthias sighed and slumped. At least he'd tried. "Fine, then, off with you! I have duties to attend to." He brushed Encanto off with a curt wave of his hand, whereupon glistened the same silver ring that adorned the fist that had just scuffed his new leather armour. For a moment he stood reflective; that was all the time Encanto needed to make good his exit.

Once outside, Encanto made his way over to where Risu stood in conversation with the young playwright and a couple of fawning theatre-lovers, signing autographs and smiling. Coughing discreetly to attract her attention, he bowed at her with a flourish and held forward the envelope he had minutes ago lifted from his brother.

"By the holies, that was close. And painful. Next time you teach me a new trick, can it be one that doesn't involve me getting hurt for a change?"

Risu smiled laconically and turned over the object in her hand in plain admiration. Then she looked up and her smile changed to concern.

"How long do you think?" she asked, "before he notices?"

Encanto took a moment in thought, stroking his moustaches. "Pretty quick. It was in his hand; I expect he was about to open it when I arrived. So, whatever you want to do..." - he waved his hand dismissively - "you have put the night's great business into my dispatch. It is well it were done quickly."

"Thank you." Risu opened the envelope and swiftly read the contents. Encanto tried to edge closer so that he might gain a peek.

"I would ask why you wanted this. I thought they were on our side?" His quizzical look, tinged with what amounted to a total lack of guile, told in his reflection the opposite of that brother he had just slighted.

Risu started, alarmed. "Quickly now, follow me. We have no time to lose!" She gathered up her dress and swift-footed herself out of the ballroom without so much as a farewell to host or guests, leaving Encanto to pick up the letter he imagined had contained nothing more than simple instructions to his brother:

*Lead a detachment of your free company to the Pallini Bathhouse.*

*Do not let them enter.*

*You will find swimming therein a singular prize which must be moved in secret to our headquarters.*

*Your discretion in this matter is appreciated.*

By the time Encanto and Risu reached the bathhouse, the mermaid had gone.

# Chapter 13

"Once again, where is your father's island?" Matthias was getting tired of the questioning and lack of answers. Surely the guild had people better suited for interrogation? As far as he had been able to tell, the mermaid could not understand anything he said or speak a single word of any intelligible tongue.

The figure shifted uncomfortably in her bindings but did not yield or speak. Her scales gleamed in the twilight, and she turned her face and hissed, revealing a row of sharp teeth.

"I'm getting nowhere." Matthias looked up at the arched window. "And it's nearly midnight."

Lacrimanta twisted and eased off a length of rope, which floated to the top as she pushed herself down the length of the long, tiled pool that occupied most of the room. Shards of what sun remained lanced the surface in places, suffusing the water with a sporadic glow.

"I think," he mused, "that you are entirely too comfortable here. Should I arrange for one of the staff to drain the pool and leave you high and dry?"

At this act, the mermaid ceased struggling and instead opened her voice in a rich, sonorous tone which resounded perfectly in the watery tomb.

"Do not go fishing for a mermaid if you don't know how to swim."

Then, silence again as her deep blue eyes looked directly into his. Here was sadness and melancholy, tinged with spite and what appeared to be a touch of regret. Not a willing actor in this, perhaps, but one who had played the part often enough because it was what was expected. One who had seen too much sorrow and loss but not enough joy.

"This water needs more salt. How long do you intend to hold me here? And I need food, real food, not plates of fruit. I hunger." She flipped over, splashing Matthias with warm water, and swam off to the other end. There she sat, cooing and calling with a voice well-versed in drawing men to a watery grave.

"Is that her aim in life?" Matthias wondered. "To lure sailors to their doom? To spread sorrow and misery among their families? Does she do this out of spite, or at the bidding of another?"

"Return me to my father's kingdom immediately. His fury when he finds my captors will be terrible in the extreme. His tears of rage and grief will become waves of pain and sorrow upon your harbour walls. How would you like to see your precious city filled with seawater, a maze of flooded streets and the drowned, bloated dead?"

Those seemed to be her last words for the evening. Matthias considered more than idly if she could follow up on that threat. Certainly, more information on the king was important to the Balance of Twilight, but what they desired most of all was the location of Farozaina and the untold riches of her father's realm.

If that was not forthcoming, well, he had his orders. For now, he was content to report back to Chiaroscuro as to the limited progress he had made. His was to do or die, not to reason, and he was paid amply for his services. It did not stop him wondering why Chiaroscuro had been so keen to make sure that letter fell into his brother's hands, but the coins in his purse was more than enough to buy his silence and cooperation.

# Chapter 14

"There was no sign of her."

I sat despondently in my kitchen, idly picking at the grapes assembled in a bowl on the table. It was still early in the morning; I had lacked any real sleep and was sporting a hangover of which any sailor would have been proud. Now it looked as though our adventure was at an end, we had been betrayed by those we thought allies.

"Did you hear me?" Risu looked concerned, her hand lifted to my cheek and raised my tear-stained, exhausted face to hers.

"I...we've lost. What can we possibly do now? What of our plans for the expedition, for the riches beyond!? What do we tell our backers? We can't possibly hope to find Farozaina without our little princess...." I tailed off, my head deep in my hands and my heart deep in despair.

"We'll think of something. It's unlikely anyone else knows what happened - we can make suitable excuses for our hurried departure from the ball."

At that moment, we were brusquely interrupted by the shuffling feet of my housekeeper.

"A message for you, just arrived. Your attendance is required immediately at the Duomo Capadomus, to further a conversation with Nonavetti. The bearer of this message indicated the urgency of the matter and the degree to which her anger at your deception can be brought to bear upon your interests." He managed to deliver this line with his customary dry sarcasm and with eyebrows raised so high they may have been mistaken for constellations.

I groaned into my cupped hands but stood nevertheless and straightened my rumpled clothes.

"I'll go alone. Who knows what she might have planned? I'll try and keep you out of it."

"I won't hear of it!" Risu replied. "I'm in this for the whole journey. But since we have two other patrons who might be circling, I will take on one of them while you charm the young starlet. It's time I returned this dress to our bountiful party hostess."

I gave a tired nod - happy to still have a confident confidant but resigned to what could be a difficult and trying day ahead of us. We resolved to meet later for supper at the Trattoria di Fonzi, which was Risu's favourite.

***

I hurried through the cobbled narrow streets and stairs until the great church came into sight. Above its sombre and sobering grey slate hung dark, rumbling clouds. Not a good sign. The cavernous interior was almost empty at this hour and in my haste, I tripped over a slab near the entrance, knocking over a chair and uttering a most unseemly oath which then echoed persistently for a number of circuits under the vaulted arches. Subtlety now lost, I caught the attention of Nonavetti who stood at the end of the nave, arms crossed, her face a contorted mask of rage and smug satisfaction. I did not see her companion until it was too late. He was a nuncio of the Salva Anima, and by the red sash which held his robe in place, he was dedicated to inquisitorial arts. He might even be a trained diviner, though the vagaries of the Salva Anima faith tended to frown on such activities these days.

I suppressed my natural urges to spit and swear and strode forward to greet them both, my gait steady but unhurried, my eyes proclaiming innocence and ignorance. I pondered my approach as I neared them - it wasn't as if acting was unfamiliar to me. I hadn't picked Nonavetti as a member of the Salva Anima faith; I'd assumed she was Sancta Sophia like many of the old families in the city whose family names still carried weight and influence. I wondered if this was a well-played bluff. The Salva Anima were concerned mostly with the behaviours in life which might taint one's immortal soul, though doctrines disagreed from duomo to duomo as to what might be considered good behaviour. I'd ridiculed their clergy in several productions.

"Pleasure to meet you, nuncio."

"I'm sure." His face pinched as if my assumed moral indecency was an assault on his nostrils. "Are you prepared to undergo the rite of immersion and emerge from the murky depths into the clean waters of clarity?" He looked down at me as if I were nothing.

"Quite." I couldn't see any divinatory tools about him, which meant that for someone outside the faith like myself, I only had to survive the scrutiny of his eyes and not any further reserves of will he could draw on. My soul might be safe after all.

\*\*\*

"You must absolutely borrow it again, if you wish to." Julietta sipped her coffee, still scalding, as Risu clasped her hands together in joy.

"That is most kind of you, given the hasty exit we were forced to make last night. I hope we did not cause too much of a stir!"

"Let them gossip," quipped Julietta, "There are more important things to concern us today."

"I had assumed as much. That is the main reason I decided to pay this visit to you."

"Pick a better mark next time. I'll not deny you your profession, but I'll not hire you either if you can't make a better effort."

That was an unexpected twist. "The story gets ahead of us, sometimes. Like a good recipe, it demands delicacy of ingredients, expertly prepared and cooked to perfection. Not like that half-baked scheme we palmed off on Buolio and Nonavetti." Risu offered a conspiratorial wink which caught the hostess's attention. "So, are you still in?"

Julietta shot back a glance that could have pierced the heart of her most ardent lover, and probably had. Then, over her face, came a devastating, all-encompassing grin which was far worse. "Naturally."

\*\*\*

"...Had the gall to perform the ceremony right there! I was beside myself." Risu listened whilst plucking at a plate of mussels in wine with a miniature silver fork. "Still, her fears are mollified, for now. I had to divulge more than she already knew, and I still don't know exactly where she got the news from, though I think we can guess the ultimate source." I was speaking too fast, still caught up in the rush of the day's pursuits. The ritual of questioning had seemed interminable, but I had been proven worthy, even if the capricious Nonavetti continued to bear a grudge fit for a pirate.

Risu had already told me of her success in talking round Julietta, so our conversation dipped as we dined. The only other business we were likely to discuss could wait for walls with less ears.

"Pardon me, but your third guest has arrived." We both looked up in surprise at the waiter, whose measure of composure eclipsed his humble surroundings. The Fonzi offered the finest seafood - according to Risu - but was by no means one of the more fashionable eateries in Lateen. I glimpsed past him to see who it might be. Naturally, it was Buolio.

"Of course it's Buolio. He owns this place." Risu stood and beckoned over to Buolio who was waving frantically to get our attention, apparently already oblivious that his waiter had done the job for him.

"I think, perhaps, that I would like to join you. I have been hearing some ugly rumours about our venture. I understand Nonavetti has already pulled out? Believe me, you won't regret that loss." He sat down gracefully in the chair that the waiter had drawn back for him and ordered a bottle of wine. "It is my understanding that the new play is a ruse. Is that correct?" When neither of us moved to deny it, he continued. "Very well. That's what's got Nonavetti's feathers so ruffled. I assume, however, that there are good reasons for the proposed voyage, nevertheless. I would like to offer my continued cooperation in return for," - his eyes rolled at this - "suitable reward. I see no reason why you need to include the others in on the secret. It's the island, isn't it? One can hardly own interests in half the dockyards and shipping in our City of Sails without gathering one's own intelligence and opinions on the subject."

"Of course! I'm sure we would be more than willing to enter into an agreement. Perhaps we can meet formally tomorrow. I'm afraid the events of the past few days have left me bereft of my senses."

"And this can stay between us?" He was most insistently pushing this point. I wondered what price he might exact from us.

"I'm afraid not." Risu interrupted. "The waiter who served us earlier isn't a waiter, he's from the Twilight. And he's heard every word."

# Chapter 15

It was at this time of heightened tension in the city that a young scholar arrived from the east, from the mountain fastnesses of Montazzura, bringing tidings of clarity, destiny, and unity. I can still recall these months later my first impressions of Paratiritis and they never fail to make me smile. One so dishevelled had never before made their way to my door and borne my humour upon his brow with such stoicism and good grace. When I first responded to the rapping, I had believed it to be Risu returned with news from the harbour and fair flung open the door, padding back into my chambers without a glance over my shoulder. Only when no footsteps followed did I turn and face the fellow framed in my doorway.

He wore robes which must once have been a fine celestian blue, with sashes of brighter cyan and darker teal. He had however clearly been subject to some of our city's seedier elements and the robes were ripped and torn in a number of places. His long black hair was uncombed and unkempt, his eyes were wide and wild. There was a thin scratch on his cheek which formed a crescent of crusted blood. I rushed back to the door to usher him in for fear that I might be mistaken for a poor host when a stranger in need came knocking. He nodded serenely and inquired as to my identity. When I responded he nodded thoughtfully and gave me the self-same look as I often gave others, studying the contours of my face, the heaviness of my eyelids and the curve of my lips. I, for one, let his eyes roam as I was embarking on a similar study. I found nothing behind those eyes, nothing in the lines of his lips which betrayed any of his intentions, only a slight tension as if a spring was coiled within him. Finally, he seemed to make a decision of sorts and, closing my door behind him, entered the hallway and set down there a small satchel, worn and weatherbeaten. Without further ado, I bade him follow me to the parlour. I was no physician, but I could at least offer him food and wine until Risu was able to take a longer look at his superficial cuts and bruises.

With my back turned to my guest while I fixed a plate of victuals and a glass of spiced wine to settle his nerves, I invited him to sit and asked for his name, which he duly gave in a passive, practised tone. When I finally turned to greet him properly, plates in hand, I laughed out loud in surprise. In a matter of moments, his countenance had been transformed - gone was the faint scratch and the light bruise, vanished the tears and stains upon the hem of his garments. He was utterly changed! Seeing my reaction, he allowed himself a faint smile and began an explanation of his metamorphosis.

"Having undertaken a journey from Montazzura to our sole port, Ohori, known as the Inkwell, and then by sea to Lateen to meet here with you, I paused upon the way in all the inns and taverns to gain a greater appreciation of what might await me once I had reached Lateen and began my investigations as to your location in the city proper. Thus I endeavoured to give some small manner of distress to my appearance, as your mountebanks and street sneaks have a reputation for regarding well-dressed foreigners as easy marks, whereas one who appears to already have survived such an encounter would be left alone and face no more weary discussions about probability or assaults on my person by thugs in dark alleys. I trust by your surprise that I have achieved a second end to my subterfuge, namely impressing upon you the skills and arts I may bring to your company. For in addition to the minor legerdemain you have already noticed, I am in fact a diviner of no small skill, reliant on the stars and the heavens both to guide my way through life. I am Paratiritis of Montazzura and I place myself at your disposal."

All this was delivered in a rapid patter with only one discernible pause for breath and followed by a sharp nod of the head which I took for an understated bow. I placed the plates on a small side-table and began a fervent round of applause; a better disguise and quick-change I had rarely seen in all my years on the stage. When I rushed forward with the intent of vigorously shaking his hand, he at first recoiled, then drew himself in and relaxed slightly and finally offered his hand in return. This was not the hand of a mere scholar, I observed, here was someone who had climbed mountains, braved elements. From his comments, my small knowledge of the easterners' peculiar philosophies and his pale demeanour I took him to be an astrologer though what had brought him to my door I could not yet imagine. Even in the heat of all the discussions in the city, I did not take him for a seeker of treasure and when he had stated with such a flourish that he could bring skills to my company I had assumed - hopefully and foolishly both - that he had meant my acting troupe.

When we were both at last seated and the viands began to dwindle on the plate, he explained what it was that had precipitated his travels from his secluded observatory in the mountains of Montazzura to the hearth of a Lateen thespian.

"Most of us rarely leave our academies, preferring a life of study and contemplation to the rigours of exposure to the elements. With but a single port, our nation is quite different from most of those on the Mare Nostrum. There are those, however, who understand that the truth is 'out there' and not bound in journals of hide and leather - at least not yet!" At this point he looked up and I realised he was expecting a laugh. When I merely looked back, he adjusted his posture and continued. Step One: know your audience and adjust accordingly. "I am an astrologer in the sense that I pay heed to the movement and passing of the great constellations by studying the heavens directly and theorise on the connections between the above and the below. I thus arranged transport from the mountaintop and followed the results of my divinations westward until I knew that the first stage of my journey was your residence in the city of Lateen and that the second journey would take us far to the west, perhaps into the Mare Lontana itself but also beneath the very waters we sail upon."

I looked as surprised to hear that latter statement as the young scholar appeared to be to make it. It was not that he seemed unsure - he brimmed with the confidence of a master in his field - but that such a possibility should have even entertained his eyes seemed to have him in a flux of perplexity.

"Naturally my assumptions on learning this were twofold: first, that I may drown on this voyage, second that there really is a city beneath the ocean. Though that supposition takes me far from the stars which are my means of understanding, nevertheless there may be unrevealed methods of divination and obscurantism within a place that manages to hide from our shipping. I therefore offer my services to you, such as they are, and implore that you take me on the sea voyage I know you are planning. I would ask that you relate to me the nature of this journey so I might further interpret my own divinations to fuller effect and with the understanding that I will not repeat a word unless it is at your direction."

"I myself," I uttered, taking a sip of dry white wine, "am both a diviner and a practitioner of legerdemain - revelation and obfuscation both. Another member of my party is also skilled in these arts. We are not lacking in diviners, it seems."

He seemed downtrodden and slumped slightly, imagining that I was about to refuse. I waved off these concerns with a friendly gesture. "But who am I to deny your quest? It seems we are to be fellow travellers on the sea of life, and I would be a fool to refuse you. First, though, you need to know what has come before. Tell me, Paratiritis, what do you know about mermaids?"

# Chapter 16

No one could agree as to where the crucial meeting should be held. Each guild offered their headquarters for the negotiations, but each offer was soundly rejected by the others as soon as the messengers arrived at their residences. A place of neutrality was eventually forthcoming - Loria University agreed to open its doors in return for a share in information received about the island and samples of new flora or fauna discovered by any of the crews. It was in this great marble edifice that representatives from all the important guilds in the city now sat, stood, jostled, argued and whispered. Chiaroscuro looked pleased with the scene as she sat at a grand round table hastily moved to the stage of the largest lecture theatre. Studies were temporarily suspended, to the consternation of the Dean of Medicine, but most students stayed anyway, impressed by the influx of the city's most influential movers and shakers.

It had been decided that everyone should speak, but no consideration had been given to the order in which this should happen. Eventually, Chiaroscuro stood, and silence fell around her.

"We know why we are gathered. The call of the sea is upon our shores, and none here would want to be the ones not to profit from the prospect. Some of us have more information than others, some of us more resources. If we all pool, we seek to gain only a margin of that believed reward. There are among us, though, those who would profit in different ways: from the possibilities of trade or diplomacy, from the knowledge that might be gained through contact with the merfolk or from we might surmise from their magic, philosophy, or technology. A fair and equal division is hardly likely. What then are we to do?" This last line was delivered with a shrug of the shoulders that was evidently mock to Matthias, who stood just behind her to the left, poised to defend her if need be. Some of those assembled appeared to take it as a genuine inquiry, others appreciated the implication that they were at an impasse which would take days of patient negotiation. I noticed myself that some seemed to relish those talks as a test of their diplomatic skills, while others looked horrified at the prospect and would rather return to their assorted guildhouses.

Buolio stood and spoke first. "I acknowledge the position put forward by the notable intelligencer but disagree with the priorities placed. Yes, there is much to gain for us all. We do not, however, all have the same to offer and some of us..." - I could not make out to whom this remark was addressed - "are incapable of estimating the value of their own contributions with any degree of veracity."

This point from Buolio drew laughter from some of those assembled, but Risu placed a cautionary arm on my wrist and whispered to me.

"Those do not sound like his words, nor would I have expected him to be the first to speak. He seemed to be less proactive at our previous encounters."

I nodded in agreement. "You think someone else guides his tongue? Who might have gotten to him?"

In response, Risu jerked her head over to where a quiet Nonavetti sat nearby, apparently enthralled by the muttered conversations that had grown up around her.

"There are other considerations to be made, of course." This came from our former hostess Juliana who had not taken a chair when one was offered but stood in a position which offered her an excellent view of the whole table and had the well-understood side effect of making her head and shoulders above those sitting. "We could argue whether we all contribute the same amount, or the same percentage of our assets, or whatever portion we are willing to offer, in exchange for whatever potential wealth, in whatever form, that might wait for us. There are too many pieces to this intricate jewellery we all desire. There may, however, be an alternate solution. We send one ship, with an agreed crew representative of us all, which minimises our costs. If that ship returns - and the risk involved would suggest an 'if' rather than a 'when' - by all means bid on each item of interest to you that the crew returns with. This ensures that we are each reimbursed in the way that is most suitable to our individual needs."

Risu and I both noticed her hand clasped to her pearl necklace at this point, an unconscious move perhaps but a telling one. Her idea seemed to gain traction around the room though and several murmured conversations struck up, with a good deal of nodding and grunting. Only Chiaroscuro looked disappointed.

"We cannot each put up an identical stake. The knowledge which my guild has gathered, in addition to the royal guest we are entertaining, puts us at the forefront of any venture. I daresay we don't need any of you at all beyond equipment which we might wish to purchase. For a very reasonable price, of course."

Buolio looked furious. "If I choose not to sell you a ship for its mere value in coin, what then? Would you hire one from Wrecker's Point and risk a crew of knaves when the stakes are so high?" He sat down with a great thump onto a red velvet cushion which threw up a cloud of chalk dust.

"I have a notion." Risu had stepped up to the table, quite unexpectedly as was evident in my eyes and heartbeat both. What was she thinking? There were several disgruntled rumblings from the floor, and several stood in protest, shaking fists. Who was this upstart who saw fit to address the assembled guilds of Lateen? Who did she represent? Those closest to her who were unfamiliar inspected her raiment closely with anxious eyes to garner any clues as to where her loyalties might lie. None of this stopped her from speaking. Rather than raising her voice to be heard, she lowered it so that others had to fall quiet just to understand her utterance.

"It is true that the Balance of Twilight holds a vital key in this venture." I wrinkled my nose a little, knowing just too well how they had come by Lacrimanta, which still smarted with me. I had trusted their generosity when I should have acted with caution. Risu did shoot over a glance, and I read in that the notion that she knew what she was doing and did not need any assistance from me. Once again, I left the situation to her ample talents.

"They are, however, not the only diviners in town. Those of us who specialise in studying the ocean know more of its secrets that you might imagine. I believe I can find the island myself and what is more I am prepared to share that understanding with you all."

If Risu deigning to address the table caused a consternation, what followed can only be described as an uproar. The room divided squarely into those who erupted in rapturous applause and those who immediately began to wonder what the price would be, or what other notion she might have in mind. I stole a glimpse at Chiaroscuro, expecting a flash of fury beneath her impenetrable mask. I was disappointed.

"If we all have the same information, we all stand the same chance of reaching the island. If that information proves false, we all lose. Should it prove correct -" Risu paused for effect, beginning to warm to her audience now. "- then who might prevail? The fastest ship, with the hardiest crew!" What better way to resolve our differences than a little competition and all rake in the coin from the spectacle provided. A race! First to get to the island and back with proof."

At this there was no argument. Each could field their own team, relevant to their particular interests. The race would bring in lots of visitors, encourage healthy competition in the markets, allow champions to prove their worth. When even Chiaroscuro nodded assent, the meeting was adjourned in favour of luncheon, while the planning for the race continued late into the afternoon.

*** 

Next morning, the guilds' decision chased the dawn rays of the sun and pierced every parlour in Lateen. As the city rose and breakfasted, hastily printed advertisements for the race were pasted onto white city walls, tacked to every tavern and trattoria. All the city was talking again of the mysterious island; crafty captains held court on the docks claiming they saw it first, smiling street sneaks and crafty merchants began to scheme. A second tide of gossip rolled over Lateen as swiftly as the first and carried the news inland on waves of hearsay.

Meanwhile, messengers were dispatched to the farthest-flung cities of the Mare Nostrum seeking willing contestants in a dangerous yet rewarding endeavour. Harbours sang to the bells of criers and the bustle of quayside hostelries. Then the sea grew calm, and the gulls stopped screeching, circling and waiting for the next storm to arrive.

# Chapter 17

Lateen, City of Sails. Foremost port of Ilforza, whose people had been the first to understand the winds and currents of the Mare Nostrum and had capitulated on that advantage ever since. The perfect place to start a maritime expedition. As dawn broke over the harbour, the sea of white calico sails shone over the glittering blue bay. The morning was all bright winter, the sun all light and no heat, the wind whipping up the last of the autumn leaves into a fierce frenzy. There were hundreds of people lining the streets and quays beyond by mid-morning, all clamouring to see the ships and their crew set off west in search of the impossible. Children fidgeted impatiently on their parents' shoulders, their mouths stuffed with lollipops, their eyes full of wonder, their hands clutching and waving flags of all colours depending on which team they currently favoured – and everyone had a favourite. In one particularly ill-reputed district, two fights broke out between rival supporters which the militia had to take time off from the docks to deal with.

I emerged from the Hotel di Lettio where Buolio had graciously put us up for the evening. Encanto followed next, squinting and shielding his eyes against the brightness of the morning. He was in good spirits, I recall, and shook hands with several supporters as he made his way through the crowd in the hotel courtyard to the throng-packed cobbles of the main thoroughfare. He reminded me of nothing less than myself some months previous; enjoying recent promotion to fame without yet being weighed down with any of the hooks, lines or nets of that fickle mistress. Wearing his finest linens and unencumbered by any possessions (these had been sent on ahead to our ship by a procession of personnel from the guild of dockstaffers), he cheerfully waved his way south to where we would meet the harbour road. Giuseppe had already left, much earlier in the morning, to make final inspections of his new ship, with all the motherly pride a mariner can muster but with an element of fussiness the same mother shows when dressing her infants for their first night at the opera.

Only Risu appeared not to be excited or moved by the cheering crowds. She walked calmly and slowly; her thin mouth fixed in a bemused grin. When a young girl burst through the assembled masses and ran forward into the road to offer her a bunch of flowers, she was taken aback with surprise but accepted them gracefully. She seemed content to let Encanto and I bask in the warmth of adoration while she remained in the shadows cast by her voluminous hooded robe.

Other hopefuls then began to emerge from their overnight stays and there was, as we rehearsed, some staged adversarial fist-waving and sabre-rattling between us. We were, after all, competitors in a great venture. Those among us who took this expedition seriously though knew that our greatest enemies were not amongst us in the pomp of this procession but further south, in the depths of the ocean and the holds of our boats. Capsizing, drowning, starving were the true opposition against which we were arrayed, and each ship had been carefully packed to the capacity and crew it would allow.

Amongst the other competitors there were several of which I had previously been unaware, but of which our genial hosts had carefully provided a minimal biography, artfully mimeographed on waxed mulberry paper and fashioned into a presentation booklet available to the crowds for a small consideration of coin. A glimpse indicated that each was accompanied with a caricature and the name of their ship. We were among the company of professional treasure-seekers, seafarers and monster slayers.

After the procession to the harbour, we all duly boarded our respective ships. Some bade farewell to loved ones on the dock, some bade welcome to their crews. Encanto stood on the gangplank and waved at the crowd, but their eyes turned to favour his brother Matthias when he rounded the quay with his crew in tow behind him. He slunk onto the ship and spent the rest of the morning in his cabin. Risu used the opportunity to perform some minor acts of legerdemain for the crowd with flash powder and theatrical smoke borrowed from our troupe's stores.

One figure stood out, high on a makeshift wooden scaffold erected high on the harbour wall, his cloak billowing in the wind: The Sindaco of Lateen was here to start the race officially. A former resident of the city's silk district who won the nomination after the unfortunate disappearance of his predecessor, he had proven so far to make the city considerably more cosmopolitan than it had been previously and the coin purses and warehouses alike swelled with foreign trade.

A great cheer went up from the mariners assembled on their respective decks. Two sailors on the Adrina produced great drums seemingly from nowhere and struck up a bawdy song dedicated to the supposed fate of that predecessor whilst apparently honouring the Sindaco's achievements.

When the applause from this had died down, the new Sindaco raised his hand for silence. Without a speech or a single word (he would have struggled to have himself heard, to be fair, above even the low murmur of the crowds, given the size of the assembly) he gave notice for us to begin. At his signal – the waving of a giant red flag in the blue morning sky – the ships all at once began to weave their way around the quays and set their sails firmly against the wind for maximum advantage. We gave a good performance for our send off, but it was clear that we were far from favourites in the running. This we hoped to turn to some small advantage, that we perhaps lulled the other crews into a false confidence of a sort. I wasn't aware of any other ship with no less than three diviners on board, each of a different tradition, and hoped that would set us in good stock as we tacked away from the quay wall and headed west along the coast.

Changing speed to take the buoy-marked channel that curved into the inner Baya Ilobo formed by the spit of Nessio, we hugged this sandy-coloured strip of land where thousands of spectators acclaimed us one more time. From there, we headed away from those channels already occupied by a multitude of smaller fishing vessels and set sail proper into the Mare Nostrum. As we saw the last of the land vanish from across the horizon, the atmosphere on ship changed sharply and the crew set themselves up in a more mournful melody to contrast the scandalous shanty we had enjoyed earlier.

And then there was nothing but the deep sea and the taste of salt and adventure.

# Chapter 18

Chiaroscuro ordered the apprentices to light the last of the braziers from the nearby torch and then dismissed them with a curt clap of her hands. The ritual communication she was about to practise required silence and solitude even though she knew the gestures by heart. Quite aside from the level of concentration it took to open the channel to her correspondent, the information she had to part in this instance she could not risk sharing, even to ranking members of the Balance of Twilight. Especially to ambitious, low-ranking members who might savour that knowledge and store it for later blackmail purposes. At least one of those apprentices she already knew had begun negotiations with an intelligencer's guild in Perigee who fancied themselves a rival, even a replacement, to her own organisation. They would have to be dealt with accordingly, of course, but all in due time. Even given the gourmet banquet of gossip laid out before her, she could only keep fingers in so many pies at one time. This matter must take priority.

As the brazier smoke began to fill the chamber, she stole a last glance at the giant water clock which took pride of place against the far wall before its mechanisms were obscured by the volume of the fumes. The time for this monthly communication had to be precise. The clock had been delivered to her apartments at the guildhall, in secrecy, for this exact purpose. Every now and then, a little light needed to be shone into dark corners, especially those dark corners in her own establishment which were caused by such shadows. When she had been approached by his agents, she had only hesitated long enough to ensure that no traps or tricks were being played. It's what she would have done, after all. What she was, in fact, still doing.

The clock itself was a thing of beauty; ancient, knotted wood which had once been ship's decking (analysis of the type of wood along with how it had been smoothed and the compounds of salts worn into the grain had confirmed this suspicion) inlaid with silver knotwork. A pair of mermaids framed the whole device and gave it form. The maid on the left smiled at her reflection in a mirror whilst the tears of the other rolled down her cheeks and formed the waves of the wooden ocean on which the apparatus sat. A great dish at the top of the device, which Chiaroscuro had taken for silver until further investigation had revealed it to be composed of the outer shell of a giant sea turtle, was polished to perfection. When she'd had the device installed (shadowy robed figures had arrived late one evening with its components and worked tirelessly and silently until dawn until they had assembled it), they had carefully arranged it to capture the light of the full moon through her roof porthole and reflect the gleam downward onto the array of delicate machinery. From her own limited understanding (her usual team of experts being unavailable for a construct which required this degree of secrecy) the water flow through the device kept a track not just of the time of day but also the lunar month including details such as the nature of the current tides – high, low, neap, spring. It was also no surprise, given the nature of her correspondent, that the water was saline.

With a swift tug on a cord next to the door to the ritual chamber, curtains rose to reveal the mirrors in the room, scintillating with reflected torchlight and flooding the area with hazy images of her black and white robes and her own mask, half smiling and half downcast. As the last glass of the water clock was filled, the filigreed mechanisms clacked into place and a scene was projected from the light of the full moon to within the great bowl of water that sat at the base of the mechanism. Via the careful arrangement of reflected surfaces in the room, this scene then filled each mirror in turn. From her selective position sat on a raised dais in the centre of the room, Chiaroscuro had a perfect view of the coral throne of the King Under The Sea.

"Greetings, Your Hadal Majesty. I hope the day finds you well." Chiaroscuro was impeccable in her delivery of the necessary honorifics, pleasantries and forms of address for everyone she dealt with. Lists and ledgers of the personal preferences of every public persona and private power across the known world filled enormous rooms in the opulent guildhall, updated meticulously by a team of trusted staff. Some were not trusted to paper and merely existed in the scheming minds of her inner circle, having been whispered by shadow courtiers or revealed by piercing light. "The tides are right."

"The tides are right" intoned the king in return. "Does your champion travel upon them?"

"My champion travels upon them." She had learned - by trial and error since no other source was available to offer information - to be polite and formal, not to give anything away. Her mask concealed her face of course - she'd been surprised the king had never asked her to remove it. "All the pieces are set in motion, the champion travels toward your realm now in your daughter's company."

"Good news. The deception" - Chiaroscuro thought she saw the king wince a little at the mention of the word - "It has been enacted?"

"It has." In the past, she would have had to bite her lip not to enthuse as to how clever she had been. That was long ago though. She didn't get where she was by revealing all the pieces in play. Instead, she merely repeated "The tides are right."

The king sensed he would get little more information from her, though in truth there was truly little more that he needed. With nothing more that needed to be said, he withdrew into the shadows surrounding his throne, leaving Chiaroscuro seemingly alone, shaking, sweating and relieved that the king had not apparently noticed precisely what she had said.

# Chapter 19

Day and night we observed the surface of the ocean, each after the other over and over with no sight of land. It is commonly spoken amongst diviners in Ilforza that day reveals and night conceals, but that is not true of the ocean. The only thing a new day revealed was the endless waters.

I was hardly drawn by the lure of prize money and had already drunk deep from the glass of glamour and the firkin of fame, yet I was far from the least attentive on board. Snatching only a few minutes for meals and a few hours for sleep, come rain or come shine, I no longer left the ship's deck. Sometimes bending over the forecastle railings, sometimes leaning against the stern rail, I eagerly scoured that cotton-coloured wake that whitened the ocean as far as the eye could see. Many times, I shared the excitement of general staff and crew when some unpredictable, uncharted, unknown island loomed large in the spyglass, but they all proved to be nought. In an instant the sloop's deck would become densely populated. But we found nothing! Nothing except an immenseness of rolling waves. Nothing remotely resembling the sketches I had made from sailor's impressions, no narwhal, or derelict shipwreck, or runaway reef or anything the least bit unearthly!

The one encounter we did have was with the Cuvier, a competitor ship which nevertheless beckoned us to draw alongside. The goodwife Marie was kind enough to allow Risu, Giuseppe,

Encanto and I to share in their evening meal, which was eaten in a celebratory style, with long trestle tables temporarily affixed to the deck. Her chef husband Paolo himself came out to join us and carved the excellent ham hocks he had stuffed with crab-apples and herb suet. Accompanied with honey-glazed carrots and pickled cabbage with sultanas, then washed down with a fine porter, the whole repast probably amounted to more than I had eaten in a week. He shared with us several recipes which I lamented later we did not have the opportunity to try.

When discussing culinary matters, his opinions were as strong as his sauces. I imagined him ruling over one of the kitchens at a fine Lateen banquet, cleaver in hand as he berated the sous-chefs on the sharpness of their knives and tasted every dish to ensure it was cooked to perfection before bellowing for the waiters to carry it to table.

When talk turned to our common goal, he laughed uproariously and admitted his ignorance of our destination. His main aim, he stated, was to delve the depths for fresh and exciting ingredients as yet unknown to the farms or kitchens, to plumb the bounty of the sea for fish, crustaceans and exotic plants alike. This would stand him in better stead in his chosen profession, and further his career and interests more than the mere fame of the explorer. Whilst we sailed the same seas, we had different harbours to call home. I exchanged some ideas and sketches of the island with him whilst Risu played with the wild-haired children that were loosed, bored, on the deck after the meal ended. We promised to share further should we meet again (which we never did, much to my stomach's disappointment) and parted amicably. Risu, who was familiar with many foodstuffs obtained from the sea, gave Paolo several pointers as to the sort of waters he might find such harvests - plains of seagrasses in the shallows where schooled vast swathes of sea life from green sea turtles to rock lobsters (both delicious) and tropical cone snails (medicinal) to toxic anemones and jellyfish. Paolo made copious notes, thanked her profusely and extended to us an invitation to visit him at his home near Peroia in a village called Violi Verdi should we survive our adventures.

# Chapter 20

Eleven days into our journey, I spied Risu and Paratiritis on deck after dark, she watching the sea and he the sky. I stood and watched them both for a while, studying their faces and movements and then approached to offer what I could to their conversation.

"There is a storm coming. You won't see it in the skies, young scholar, only in the waters."

"There are no storms without clouds! It is they who are the harbingers of rain and lightning, not some shells you press to your ear for an answer, nor some reading of fish bones. It is to the skies we must turn if we want warning of ill-weather. And the skies" – he gestured jerkily – "are more clear here than on the highest mountains of Montazzura!" The constellations and their movement tell us our location as well, we are guided more by the stars than the waters." He folded his arms into his robes, not in frustration but merely in anticipation of her response.

"To the stars? What do constellations tell you, young scholar, that the waters do not? Do they give the location of our destination? By all means, then, direct our course!"

I drew up alongside them and offered each a hot buttered rum fresh from the galley. Paratiritis accepted it gracefully and sipped at it quizzically. Risu played with the foamy top, licking the froth from her fingers.

"Surely" I interjected, "We should not discount any source in our studies. I am practised in the study of liminal times and spaces, those borders between land and sea, sky and earth, day and night. It's why I named my troupe Dusk Till Dawn. Must not a fusion of both approaches be desired as a consideration for all divinatory magics? Do we not seek answers from the horizon, a conundrum which we can see but never reach?" I thought this response very clever, indeed it had been an underlying theme of one of my earlier plays. However, both diviners turned their necks and rounded on me swiftly, though Risu downed her mug of rum first.

"The sea must be approached, though, from the land or from the heavens". Paratiritis looked upward to his precious stars. As above, so below. If we are to make progress in our quest, the future will reveal itself to us in the night sky."

"Not so," Risu chimed in, "the sea can be approached from the sea, depths from shallows. This shell – she held up the conch Paratiritis had earlier mocked – allows me to commune with the seabed itself. There can be no place further from the heavens you study."

Paratiritis looked up in wonder at this. I could see his eyes light up and I must confess mine did also. Who could have thought Risu would have command over such a powerful object! Was it this which guided her true dockside divinations about the nature of the seas and skies, when storms might come and whether winds would will us becalmed? He reached out a hand to hers and she looked long into his eyes before handing him the shell over for inspection. As he held the large conch to his ear, eager for it to divulge its whispered words, I saw Risu swallow a smirk.

"Foolish boy! Wretched watcher of the skies! Do you think you can call on me?" The conch bellowed out, causing Paratiritis to drop it and his rum-mug alike and stagger backwards onto a barrel.

Risu laughed and I joined in, silently adding ventriloquism and quirky humour to my growing mental list of Risu's talents. She would make a fine player if she would forego her dock clientele and tread the boards. I knew more than a few troupes who would be glad for the addition of one with such natural showmanship, even before her skills at legerdemain and divination were taken into account. Paratiritis recovered quickly and stood stoically, then to our surprise joined in with our laughter. The three of us stood there on deck, bemused crew busying themselves around us, laughing and discussing philosophy until dawn began to steal away those precious night jewels above us and we returned to our cabins, all richer for the sharing.

# Chapter 21

Since the days and nights in the midst of the ocean were passing by uneventfully for the most, I dedicated myself to learning everything I could about my new environment in order to be of more immediate use and as fodder for future fantasies on the stage. Giuseppe showed me the ropes and bade me practise at their tying and untying until my hands began to chafe. Risu took it on herself to lecture me on all fashion of flora and fauna which inhabited the ocean, their migratory patterns and feeding habits. Paratiritis, ever the patient tutor, gave me nightly discourses on the nature and pattern of the stars and how they were useful in divination and navigation both. By the end of two weeks, I considered myself an expert mariner - in thought if not in deed. The crew still laughed at my occasional mistaken terminology but bore my attempts to learn their trade with good humour. In return, I gave a series of amusing monologues and character studies and played the flute for many a hornpipe.

It was just when I thought I had learned everything I could about the sea when we encountered three phenomena in quick succession that led me to nail my ignorance to the mast and go back to spending my time writing an account of our journey and keeping watch out for our island destination.

The first such wonder came upon us at the setting of the sun on the seventeenth day of our voyage. Scientific understanding having not yet reached the point where such marvels of nature are routinely classified and comprehended, I shall refer to it as 'The Milky Sea' until minds immeasurably superior to mine measure the mention of it in my memoirs. I was leaning against the taffrail, sketching the sunset over the sea with its glorious reds and oranges spilled out over a plain of pure blue when I first spotted it and called out to the others. I spied in the distance ahead a number of soft white lights bobbing in the ocean which I first mistook as the reflection of the stars above which had just begun to set the stage for their nightly performance. (In due fact, it was the stars I was waiting for since Paratiritis had commissioned from me a series of illustrations of the visible constellations from our current position, being further south and west than he or his fellows from the observatory had ever ventured. It would spark debate as to the nature of the heavens and their relation to the world, he explained in his rapid-fire reportage.)

By the time the others had made their way over, we had advanced to the point where we were among the lights. It had also become clear that several of them had swum out to greet us. Paratiritis gazed at them admiringly and began trying to pinpoint patterns in their positions, his mind racing with ideas of gathering them up in a net and setting them in the roof of his academy as an academic reminder of the stellar scenery by which he plied his craft. Encanto got excited at the sight of a dead crab, so to him this luminous display was a gift that kept giving. He raced from deck to deck calling out in childlike wonder, leaving Risu and I alone to contemplate the poetic beauty of our surroundings as we steered forward through the softly lit sea and wondering as to what caused them to shine and whether they were an ominous omen or merely a majestic mystery. The ship was surrounded now with these little lights, all bobbing gently on the waves around us. I must have waxed poetic at some stage about capturing one of the sea-stars, as one was taught in tales about the capture of the moon in a lake. Risu smiled gently, removed her robe in one clean gesture and then dove overboard amongst them. I was shocked at first - the studies I had undertaken at her direction had been full of cautionary notes about the multitude of poisonous and venomous creatures and yes, even plants, which inhabited the ocean depths and shallows alike. It took me a few clear moments to realise that this must be a spectacle she had seen before. I was similarly shocked when she surfaced, a tiny globe of light in her hand, and shot me a smouldering smile. I am no stranger to impetuity, but never before have I dived from a moving ship into waiting waters merely to enjoy the company and wonder of another, and never may I do so again. We swam around each other in ever-decreasing circles, splashing and playing in the seductive shimmer of the sea-lights until our lips reached each other and our bodies entwined, just as the sun dipped fully below the horizon and left us to our coy caresses and I gazed fully for the first time into her eyes.

# Chapter 22

When we awoke the next morning, the sun was already high over the yardarm. Risu leaned over me for the bottle and we shared a loving cup of wine before surfacing from the cabin to greet the remains of the day. The lights were still all about us, shining less now they had the sun for competition. Just over the horizon lay the second in the series of strange sightings which our expedition encountered. The pearlescence which had precipitated our passion had passed and shortly after the sea began to swirl in a most unwholesome manner. Following this experience, which had crew and captain alike on edge, there floated toward us a growth of wave born weeds which I have since dubbed the red tide. These gave the ocean a horrific blooded look quite different to the spectacular reds of the sunset. Among this living, thriving mass of algae were the remains of several sea creatures, cleaned to the bone by the fermenting flora. The captain, forever a superstitious and impressionable sort, barked out a series of swift commands to pin sails, tack round and make away from this strange sensation. I should confess that my recent training in all things nautical fairly escaped my faculties when we were presented with a clear and present danger such as that posed by the red tide and the approach of the third phenomenon which lied at its centre, drawing us irrevocably into its great maw; the maelstrom. The closer we got, despite the best efforts of those mariners more masterly than myself, the more panicked I became. An adventurous journey is one thing; to be eliminated before the ending of an expedition is quite another. The churning of the great whirlpool now caused a secondary sensation from the bloody blooms; they gave off a light, red mist which rose gently from the growth and moved, mindlessly, malevolently, toward the deck where we stood.

Risu appeared beside me at that point; I had no idea until then that she had left, transfixed as I was by mortal fear of our predicament. She passed me a grog-soaked rag and held it over my face. When I began to gag, she pressed it firmer. "The mist is toxic; it's caused by spores in the algae released by the churning of the sea this close to the pool. Keep this there, it will help reduce the potency of the poison. Help me pass the remainder among the others." So we went about the business of forcing sailors to inhale rum, which, whilst they are frantically running around decks and climbing sails is a much harder task than you might imagine. Two poor crew that we had not spotted in time began to choke as the mist seeped over the deck and coiled into their throats. Within seconds, they had succumbed to the red weed and, with a slow, strangled scream, began to shudder and shake as if some fit had overcome them. Before we could reach them, they were both dead on deck, their faces contorted into a hideous mask of pain and fury. We have Risu to thank for the fact that these were the only two casualties that day, and the captain to thank for staying our course under immense duress. As we were drawn in further toward the centre of the maelstrom, the ship buckled and tossed but not once did the wheel leave his hands or the look of determination vanish from his face. The swirling seas sucked us in closer to its centre, where there was no more red tide but a fair flotilla of flotsam. With horror, I noticed amongst it the peacock figurehead from the Cachalot on which one of our monster-hunter competitors had set sail. His thirst for glory had been inadequate against the very hunger of the ocean itself.

Terror seized my fevered, fanciful imagination at that point, beyond that which I had experienced before. I found myself thinking the absolute worst, how the hopes of our journey might be dashed against the rocks of reality, how soon after finding love so suddenly and unexpectedly the wretched waves would drive us from each other's embrace. I imagined for a fleeting moment that the maelstrom might devour us whole and deposit us on a foreign shore. It took the solid hold of Encanto to prevent me from being catapulted over the edge of the rail into the storm itself. "Get a grip! All hands on deck includes you, playwright!" I looked around frantically for Risu but could not see her anywhere; the bile and panic rose again in my throat as my emotions threatened to choke me. Then, from above, a crewman hurtled past us to his doom from where he had been trying to strike down the mainsail. I snapped back into the waking world and endeavoured to take his place. If I were to die in this moment, if the last boards I trod were the deck of the Dolfiena, then so be it. I fair flung myself toward the rigging and began an ascent to where I could release the sail from the hold the storm had on them. The ship tossed precariously from side to side, and I nearly lost my balance twice whilst jumping over whipping ropes and loose barrels while I made my way to the mainmast.

The ship was after all a stage, where we were playing out this melodrama and it was time for the curtain to fall on this particular episode. I made a check that the little knife Giuseppe had given me during our knot lessons was firmly tucked into my belt sash. Whilst others were buffeted across the deck whilst trying to hold their footing, I grasped the lowest handholds on the mast and began my ascent, teeth gritted in a fervent determination.

It was not easy going, and I had not expected it to be. The further I climbed the greater the toss from side to side as the mast lurched precariously. Crashing waves and biting wind lashed constantly across my face; twice I nearly faltered in my footing; twice my hands failed to clench the holds on the slippery mast. By perseverance and inner reserves of fortitude I barely knew I had, I had reached the point where I could begin to sever the ropes that held the sails in place. Had I been tempted instead to let the sail slack by regular means, it would have taken too long. I cast a glance down at the deck and could see Risu looking straight back at me. My heart skipped a beat and my resolve strengthened. Understanding what I was about to do, she began shouting at the others to clear the deck, struggling to be heard over the noise of the storm.

By the third rope, I had lost grip on my knife completely. I watched in horror as it slid out of my wet hands and clattered through the rigging out of sight in the spray of water. The sail still held. Grabbing a loose rope and with no further thought for my own safety I swung to the starboard yard spar and made fair work of the remaining ropes using only the strength remaining in my bare hands. I was exhausted and exasperated both, but here was adventure! From swinging across a stage to swinging in the rigging! I believe to this moment that the only way I managed to hold on and keep focus was by dint of casting myself chief protagonist in this maritime narrative, imagining the scene would end when I dictated it so with my success. It appears this tactic worked. With an almighty creaking, the sail and yard arms gave way and crashed to the deck. With naught for the wind to catch on, only the current drove us further inward. How that would be overcome I did not know; I was dangling from the mast by one hand, flushed with success. The curtain had fallen.

# Chapter 23

I awoke later on the deck, at night. There was no sign of the great whirlpool which had placed us in peril. My head ached from...well, I wasn't exactly sure, but it was no ordinary hangover. I almost longed at that point - while trying to rise and stretch my aching limbs - for my former life on land. Those days seemed so long ago that it was difficult to recall the scenes I had directed and starred in, they were all ablur in misty memory of my former vocation. I put this initially down to the lump on my brow - surely the proximal cause of my aforementioned malady - but the more I tried to think about it, the more those tides of memory receded from me. Eventually, I chalked it up to adrenalin, adventure and exhaustion. If I'd have realised then what was actually happening, the rest of our sojourn would surely have proceeded very differently.

The vagaries of an ocean voyage being what they are, no sooner had we escaped the violence of the storm and the whirlpool, then we were set upon by the exact opposite. We found ourselves utterly becalmed. There was not enough wind to catch the mainsail and it did not help that our sails were in a state of disrepair after our earlier adventure. No winds filled our tattered sails, no currents carried us. The weeds that courted the Dolfiena were those similarly vomited forth by the tempest's hunger, not red this time but green sargassum. Amongst this knotted kelp were the regurgitated remains of ships that had fallen prey to its voracious appetite, and amongst that flotsam were a couple of ships who were strangely intact. Clearly, they had not weathered the storm such as we had, and I was at once both curious and nervous in wonder as to what fate might have befallen them. Risu seemed to appreciate my concerns and came to stand beside me on the foc'sle, linking her arm in mine and offering me victuals from a small wooden bowl (dried beef dipped in port - rather good if a little salty for my palate).

"They're not victims of the storm, my love. They're victims of this place. 'Where winds do not blow, no sailor should go'. All these ships" - she outstretched a tanned arm, shells dangling from her fine wrist and sparkling in the strong sunlight - "were trapped here, becalmed as we now are and did not feel the sea breeze on their necks again until their dying days. They ran out of food, or fresh water, or fell among themselves in fear and alarm. Ghosts of mariners past haunt these wretched wrecks, those good people who signed up for an adventure only to die at the hands of its very antithesis - no excitement, no movement, just malingering fear and panic until madness sets in. Catharsis, inaction and death."

I turned to meet her gaze. It was unusual for her to be so introspective, even maudlin. She assured me it was nothing, but as this assertion was accompanied by her uncoupling her arm from mine, I remained unconvinced. Still, I said nothing further, and we both stood there silently, watching the gentle bobbing of the waves and hoping for a change in the weather before we were called for an audience with the captain.

Since we were at a loose end, the captain and Giuseppe had ordered the crew to check and repair the ropes and rigging and sew up the holes in the canvas, which occupied them for a time while we discussed our predicament. There were some suggestions that we could salvage fresh canvas from the corpses of those great vessels which floated in this watery grave, but superstitious sentiment at the possibility of ghosts and worse put paid to the plan. Whilst the crew set about their work, we retired to the captain's cabin for urgent discussion of our dilemma.

The captain spoke her piece first. "This is a fine mess, no mistake. The crew are tired, strained from the storm and weeks of searching in vain. No amount of rowing can avail us in our exhaustion, not upon seas this high. Now we cannot move; there is little action that can be taken to remove ourselves from the situation other than to await the winds. Judging by those who have been here afore us, I don't trust they'll come, mark my words. A doom awaits us here. She sank her head low to the table, to the point where her head hung at a precarious angle and the tips of her hair came close to swimming in her cinnamon oatmeal.

Giuseppe spoke in unison with the captain. He'd heard tell of these places - be they called doldrums, or the more alarmist ships graveyards. Up until now, he had never thought them to exist though - he rubbed his beard thoughtfully - up until recently he would have said the same about unnaturally turbulent whirlpools, poisonous red algae or opalescent luminous sea blooms. Or, come to that, unknown floating islands or mermaids. Strange times were upon us. Neither of the most experienced seafarers had any mundane solution to our woes other than to hoist all sails and count what blessings they had left remaining.

It fell to the remainder of us then - Risu, Paratiritis and I - to consider whether there may be any other means of release we might divine from our predicament. There was little to be garnered from such a discussion though. After an hour of back-and-forth, we had exhausted all avenues open to us, just as the mariners had with the mundane. Risu resolved to perform some minor weather divinations but when Paratiritis requested he might be permitted to watch, Risu dismissed him with a firm shake of the head. When I too ventured an interest, she smiled but asked that she be allowed to retain some privacy in the matter. It was, after all, a case of professional secrecy to divulge the manner in which she earned her principal coin. I muttered agreement but felt chastised and disappointed all the same.

So, the reaction set in. At first, discouragement took hold of crews' minds, opening the door to disbelief. A new feeling appeared on board, made up of three-tenths shame and seven-tenths fury. The crew began to refer to themselves as 'credulous fools' for being hoodwinked by such a tale and imagined the whole voyage was doomed if not cursed and grew steadily at once more despondent and more furious. The mountains of arguments

103

amassed over the previous seasons collapsed all at once, and each now wanted only to return. The most enthusiastic supporters of the undertaking now became its most energetic opponents. Only two of those on board seemed immune to this malaise of the mind, the stoic, meditative Paratiritis and the relaxed, smiling Risu.

The futile search could not drag on much longer. The Dolfiena had done everything it could to succeed and had no reason to blame itself. Never had a crew shown more patience and zeal. There was nothing to do but go home - this was realised from the bowels of the ship up to the topmost sail - and finally the news came crashing over the captain's table where we were enjoying a singular luncheon of cracked crab. A number of the crew - senior officers among them - awaited behind the door while a spokeswoman was nudged forward with a list of terms and demands.

It was Risu who stepped forward in response, surprising Encanto and I alike. "Three more days," came her reply. "Give us three more days. If at that time we have shook our way free of the doldrums but not found Farozaina, there is no mariner worth their salt who would not agree that we should bank and set sail back to Lateen, should the wind and waters will it."

The crew grumbled but agreed to her terms. I began to realise just what power the diviner wielded over those who depended on the sea, how much stock they took in her simple charms and divinations. They trusted her in a different way to the loyalty they placed in their captain, different to their own ambitions and the assault on their pride at being duped by these fanciful tales of a lost island of treasure. She simply said, and it was so. The captain and Giuseppe too remained silent over their dessert, shooting glances at each other and lowering their heads. Encanto and I continued talking until late as he told another story of his adventures, this time in Segura. Paratiritis wandered out to the deck to check on his precious stars. When Encanto's tale finally ended, only Risu remained, watching us whilst sloshing the remainder of her wine around in her glass, contemplative and sleepy. Encanto turned to her.

"You had better be right, you know,". He waggled his finger pointedly at her. "We'll be lucky to still be alive in three days. I sense trouble brewing."

Risu turned to meet his gaze in full, with deep penetrating eyes. "Yes, I had better be right. We only have enough fresh water for two days." With that, she drained her glass and left us both in the cabin, dumbstruck and nervous about what would kill us first.

# Chapter 24

A full day passed with no change in the weather; the mood darkened, but not the sky. Further meetings were as fruitless as the mess now was, having almost depleted our stocks of food as well as the life-giving fresh water. We despaired utterly of redeeming the situation. Mutterings continued amongst the crew, whispered out of earshot. Glances full of daggers were shot in our direction. It would only be a matter of one more missed meal before things would come to a head.

The crowd gathered outside the captain's cabin, as we knew they would, shouting and hollering for us to turn sail and head for the nearest shore. Several knives and daggers sparkled and glinted in the noon day sun as the mass of bodies pressed in around the door, clamouring for the captain to hear their pleas.

They were interrupted by Encanto beating a plank loudly on an empty barrel. Standing on a crate which had formerly held the last of our salted beef, his voice rang out rich and clear as he raised it in song and the crew stood, rapt and attentive.

Now he had their attention, he seemed unsure momentarily as to what to do with it. His eyes widened and he uttered a low, dry rasp. Finally, he gave a nod, presumably only to himself as if he had decided on a course of action, come what may.

"I'm no seafaring man, that much is plain." He shifted uncomfortably from side to side against the gentle rise and fall of the deck as if to emphasise it.

"But I'm no stranger to danger; I've fought against Carini pirates on their own shores and taken my share of scars, stories and treasures in equal measure."

There was a general hubbub amongst those gathered. Several more of the crew came over to listen or stood stock still whilst swabbing and pricked up an ear.

"Let me tell you this truth, plain and simple: Amor Fati. Love your fate, brothers and sisters. No, not like the stoics of the south who accept everything that comes their way with expressions that could sour wine. Stare danger in the face and laugh at its impotence. Perhaps we don't all survive this voyage. Perhaps none of us do. We'll still be legends! Maybe one day someone will find this abandoned ship and whispers of our endings will haunt every tavern in Ilforza. Maybe a message in a bottle we toss over the side washes up on a distant shore, a disturbing lesson for some enterprising beachcomber."

"Now, I don't think that's what's in store for us, not today. That's not challenging my fate - I just don't think it's our fate to languish here forever until our brains are fevered from lack of drink and even the scrawniest among us begin to look like the most succulent hams. I live every day as if it might be the last. That's what makes life worth living! The childish wonder of it all. The thrill of the chase. The ringing sound of steel on steel. The need to know what's just beyond that horizon. And you know what? Fate doesn't snatch me away. It finds me too entertaining to watch."

"So, from soldier to sailor, that's my advice. If there be no wind to raise the sails, let us fill them ourselves with the sound of our laughter! Let our defiance be the breeze which frees us from defeat. If there be no spirits to raise our spirits, let us raise them ourselves and be the better for it. Who's with me?"

As the crew settled to a rousing cheer and an encore, we felt the Dolfiena lurch beneath us and then, for the first time in days, felt a cool breeze on our necks. It soon escalated and billowed the sails back to life with its precious kiss. Amor Fati had somehow won where our divinations had failed. Fate smiled on Encanto, it seemed. Whether it was laughing at him or with him didn't seem to matter in that instance. What mattered was that we got through.

# Chapter 25

For the next two days, we were shrouded in a thick bank of fog that rolled in overnight and clung to us like barnacles. We sat and shivered, repairing the rest of the damage as our captain - with Risu's help - tried to navigate using only the currents as a guide. If the sun still shone above us, it did so in mockery of our fate. It seemed we were to have no respite from ill-fortune and the spirits of the crew were lower than the floor of the ocean. We persevered, further rationed the food and water - which dampened spirits yet more - and continued regardless. Even Encanto looked despondent, his moustaches drooped with misty moisture and grim tidings. We were only no longer at risk of mutiny because none had the force of will remaining to raise arms. Then, on the afternoon of the third day, it began to lift. It did not appear that we had sailed out of it, more that it had grown as weary as the rest of us and wandered off in search of somewhere more fun. The sun shone brilliantly overhead, the waters clear beneath us, their salty tang in our mouths and the winds in our hair. This was the simple adventure I had hoped for - the mere thrill of the high seas and days spent watching dolphins leaping along behind us.

"Ship ahoy!"

My reverie was soon interrupted by the scene on the horizon once the fog had bidden us farewell. Risu lent me her spyglass, but that only served to further the horror that was unfurling.

109

"Two ships attacking another," I proclaimed breathlessly, "It's hard to tell who through all the smoke and fire."

The captain looked through her own instrument, which was similar to Risu's but made of solid brass. "Those are Carini pirate vessels." I looked intently again, desperate to understand what was happening.

"You can tell," interrupted Paratiritis, who stood calmly next to us, his arms folded in the sleeves of his many-layered robes, "because of the extra front sail - the jib. It's a thin foresail because they sail stormier seas, and a thinner foresail means that it's harder to be blown off course. Also, they are flying the red flag which dockyard gossips say is dipped in the blood of the slain - a ridiculous notion as that would take considerable time and effort and add weight to the canvas - but a rumour that persists, nonetheless. Also, because, as I'm sure you can see through your spyglass, they are swarming with pirates. Furthermore, the ship they are attacking is evidently, given the colours flown, is none other than the one belonging to our fellow racers from Ilforza - I can just about make out the three golden barrels of the Reverio cartel. That is the Elmo's Fire."

We all looked at him in awe and he shrugged effortlessly. "I'm used to looking at objects a lot further away than the horizon." He turned to the captain. "Since our own colours are tied to the mast and they have no doubt seen us as clearly as we see them, I suggest we make an immediate course change to render all assistance."

The captain nodded furiously in agreement and immediately began shouting orders. The ship lurched a little to starboard and the rowing speed was doubled, all in a matter of moments and to the thumping of a heavy drum to mark time. We closed quickly, but not quick enough. One of the pirate ships - the shape of the bird on its flag marked it out as the Albatross - moved hard to intercept us while the other finished off the Elmo's Fire, now half aflame and half submerged. I bade those poor souls' swift passage to the realms beyond as we readied ourselves for battle. By the time we were close enough to engage, the second ship - identifiable by its name engraved on the side as the Ghost Shark - had broken off from the doomed Elmo and began circling, ready to close in and join the Albatross.

If we had hoped to make swift work of the one ship before the other was close enough to be a threat, we were sadly mistaken. Many of the crew were still busy with the oars, of course, until the point at which we might be boarded. That left barely a handful of us facing the pirates, whose rowers were slaves and whose skills with the bow exceeded ours. I fastened a bolt to my crossbow and with it shot the Albatross, only to duck at the volley of return fire from the pirates. Reloading, I made a second attempt and caught one of them square in the jaw. Even over the crashing of the waves and the shouts of our crew, I could hear him scream as he hit the deck. We decked more than a score, all told, but in return they surely took out more of us and drew close enough to board. They did so with remarkable vigour and alacrity, as it was later

111

explained to me that the rig of a Carina pirate vessel is designed entirely for speed and combat more than our own more mercantile Ilforza ships. Our own vessel, the Dolfiena, had a huge cargo hold - the contents now largely depleted, of course - and was designed for the long ocean voyage we had expected. We had already suffered much damage, more than the Elmo had been able to deal to the Albatross, but now we came into our own. Each of our remaining crew was an experienced sailor and soldier, more than a match one-on-one for a corsair as they discovered to their chagrin. This was a fight we could win!

I dropped the crossbow on a nearby barrel after shooting one of the boarders clear between the eyes, leaving a stunned look on his face as he toppled backwards into the deep, taking two more pirates with him as he grabbed out in terror for a handhold. Closing with my dagger I stood between Encanto and a soldier named Adrienne, whose long hair was wisely wound into a tight bun and who stood sure-footed with a mighty Bhuj in her hands. We three saw off each pirate that closed with us, as I cast my eye around the deck on the lookout for any officers. When I spied one, I made a signal and we cut a swathe across the deck, slick now with blood and brine both, as we drew close to where he was barking orders. With a snarl, he was upon us and took Adrienne down with a single powerful blow from his glaive before turning his attention to Encanto. This was a pattern the soldier understood - his footing had grown surer after weeks at sea and he moved with a speed in defiance of his bulk. I could hear the clang of steel on steel around us but dared not let my gaze wander from the opponent who now stood before us. When he moved, Encanto intercepted him easily and knocked him to the deck. Before we could close, though, he was back on his feet and spitting curses. From somewhere to port, I heard a zing and a thud, then a grunt as Encanto took an arrow to the thigh. The flow of blood would slow him down eventually, so I made a series of quick slashes designed to occupy and disorient the officer rather than wound him while Encanto summoned up the strength to carry on. His eyes closed momentarily and then he was at one with his sword - a flurry of blows raked long, deep cuts into the chest and belly of the enemy and as he fell, I dared to take a look around at how everyone else was faring.

Our own captain was holding her own against two more pirates, with three dead at her feet, but was showing signs of tiredness. Ribbons of red ran down her sleeves and a vicious cut on her face would make an impressive scar story if we survived. Paratiritis and Risu fought back-to-back with long quarterstaffs which they swung in low, lively arcs. They kept the enemy at bay but little else. I shouted across to Encanto that we should help them, but he pointed instead over to the deck rail. "We should stop any more of those dastards getting onto the ship - if we can do that, the crew can deal with those that remain here. Follow me!"

As we made our way across the deck, I am ashamed to say that I had all but forgotten the Ghost Shark in the heat of battle. It was much closer now and from the speed even I could tell it was set to ram. What ungrateful wretches would ram a ship with their own kind already on board?! I could only assume that the surviving captain would be the one to assign the bounty and to the depths with the rest. I grabbed Encanto's cuff and tugged it hard, turning his gaze to the Ghost Shark which was now only metres away.

Any exclamation or curse we made at that point was drowned out by the cracking and splintering of wood, the crashing of rigging, the screams of horror and the waves of despair that washed over the deck. Pirate and mariner alike failed to brace for the impact and cluttered across the deck like toy soldiers tossed across the table by a petulant general. I lost sight of the others as I clung to the deck rail until my strength gave out and I felt the sharp, cold embrace of the ocean. My lungs filled, my eyes closed, my dreams dashed. We were lost.

# Chapter 26

When beholding the tranquil beauty of and brilliancy of the ocean's skin, one forgets the tiger heart that pants beneath it. His Hadal Majesty was such a heart, and he was eager for reports from his captains. A procession of them arose from the pool at the centre of the throne room, each with news for their ruler. One by one, with grave and respectful tones, they bobbed up and down in the water as they delivered their messages.

"The Cachalot succumbed to the maelstrom, O King, all hands lost. The Tides are High."

"The Jigger is wrecked on a faraway island, O King. The Tides are High."

"The Pride of Invidia is trapped in the ship's graveyard, O King. The Tides are High."

"The Bridport Dagger lies on the ocean floor nearby, O King. The Tides are High."

"The Grand Cuvier no longer seeks us, O King. Its hold is filled with our bounty, and it returns to harbour. The Tides are Low."

"The Rosmarus makes way to seas uncharted, O King. They are far off course for Farozaina. The Tides are Low."

"The Clupea has arrived safely, O King, and its crew are being entertained. The Tides are High."

"The Elmo's Fire is lost to the pirates and to fire, O King. The Tides are High."

"The Dolfiena is also lost to the pirates, O King. Their crew are receiving assistance from an expected source. The Tides are High."

"Well spoken. You are dismissed." With a bow and a sudden dive, the captains descended in unison back to the depths from which they had come.

"Mauvid, what of our special guest?"

"She has arrived safely in the manner you set out and awaits you within your antechamber, O King."

"Excellent. I will see her now - please bid her to enter through the curtain of kelp."

"As you wish."

The king spent long moments alone, deep in thought. Here was one he had recruited as an ally in this venture, but one he felt certain would betray him. But not yet, not yet. Not until she believed she had everything she wanted.

A shadowy form emerged from the end of the room, her footfalls echoing eerily across the marble floor.

"Greetings, your majesty. It is an honour to be summoned to meet you in person."

"Well said. Welcome, then, Chiaroscuro of the Balance of Twilight. Welcome to Farozaina."

# Chapter 27

Once the crowd had waved the racing ships from the Lateen harbour, Chiaroscuro - quite normally as busy and organised as one might expect the head of an intelligencers' guild to be - had gone simultaneously into hiding and overdrive. Guild associates and messengers bearing information were dismissed at the entrance to her rooms by officious grim guards who permitted no procrastination, tolerated no trouble. These were the elite of the Sarabande Free Company, whose leader just happened to now be the guild champion. It might have seemed to outsiders to be an odd decision to make when she already had a number of personal guards on service at the guild. They were unfortunately more prone to corruption, however. When she returned, she would have to clean house and deal with her rivals within the guild and without, but that was a matter for another day. With the knowledge and power she was about to accumulate, that would be much less of a problem than previously. This opportunity was not one to be missed, not after all the diligent research that lay locked in the ledgers, safely behind those guards.

She made her way apprehensively to the apparatus at the far end of the chamber, from which slow trickles of seawater perpetually dripped into waiting bowls and from thence drained away to some place unknown. Apprehensive because this was the only unpredictable element in the whole affair, the only part of the process to which she did not know all the particulars. Whilst she had used this device previously to communicate with the entity known as His Hadal Majesty, what she was about to attempt was quite different. If she understood the instructions clearly, she would be able to manipulate the energies of the artifice to travel directly to Farozaina and speak with him in person. Such potent magics had not been seen before in the lands around the Mare Nostrum except in concert with ancient magic of unknown origin, relics of the ruined lands their people had left behind to the east. Some of the scrollwork on the clock she had imagined were old Aritenae in design, but different, twisted. So older, perhaps, but impossible to decipher even given the extent of her knowledge-bringers.

She waited patiently for the correct hour. When the mermaid fountains tipped and began to pour, she gathered her senses and her garments and walked slowly forward into the waiting water.

# Chapter 28

I began gasping for air and tried unsuccessfully to surface. What I might hope to achieve should I manage to reach it I had no idea. In all likelihood, the pirates were scouring the surface looking for survivors to pick them off or take them as potential slaves. I dismissed the terror of this thought - one thing at a time. First write the script, then build the set. I peered through the turbulent water around me to see who else might be there, but I saw nobody. Hampered by clothes that were as restricting as a cloak of lead, I was managing to swim with only the greatest difficulty.

Suddenly a great force behind me knocked me aside. I felt lithe hands tug at my shirt and lift me while the force that had been behind me was suddenly under me and carrying me upward. I sat on something solid; I knew not what until we had leaped out of the water, and I had a chance to breathe again.

The experience that followed - more than any other - is one that I will always remember with joy in my heart. Around me, great spumes of foam erupted and sprayed into the air. Breaking through from the depths were a group of dolphins (Paratiritis would later correct me to use the proper group name, which is a 'pod'), many of which bore upon their backs an exhilarated, anxious and terrified member of our crew. Giuseppe clung to his for dear life, Adrienne - barely conscious - was supported by Encanto. The arms wrapped around me from behind were certainly those of Risu. Further away I could just make out some of the crew from the Elmo's Fire. Our rescuers sped us away to the south until the wreck of our ship was a distant speck on the horizon. We spent the next two hours on a white-knuckle dolphin ride through gently undulating waters, lulled occasionally into a near-slumber by the gentle rocking rhythm.

It had not occurred to me to question at that point where they were taking us until much later, when an over-excited Encanto shouted at me and began gesticulating wildly. "Land! We're here, we're here at last!" And there, just coming into sight above the gently bobbing waves, was the island of Farozaina.

***

Our aquatic companions swam us close to the sandy shore whereupon we collapsed with exhaustion and elation alike. Finally, dry land - and what's more - uncharted land in these territories which very likely meant we had at long last landed on the fabled isle we had set forth to discover so many weeks ago. We took time to relax and unwind while we could, reacquainting ourselves with having solid ground to walk on. Many of the crew ventured up the beach as far as the tree line and returned with fruits so exotic even the finest restaurants in Lateen would have trouble identifying them - succulent, mouthwatering melons the size of Encanto's head, green fruit with a spiky casing which tasted of toffees, and bunches of ripe bananas. This being the first food we had eaten in over a day, we made quite the meal of it before setting up a camp on the beach, determined to be at full strength before we decided on how best to explore the island's interior. As we sat around our little campfire, gazing up at the starlit sky, I noticed Risu standing alone further down the beach, staring out at the sea. I made a quiet approach so as not to disturb her thoughts; as I got closer, I could see that she had been crying. What I supposed were tears of joy, however, were not borne out by the expression on her face. I placed a hand gently on her shoulder and she looked at me intently.

"Whatever is wrong?" I asked. She fidgeted slightly, escaping my grasp.

"It's nothing, really. It's just... now that we're here I..."

"We have company!" bellowed Encanto. Forty or fifty figures, moving in quickly. I turned but was immediately met with a spear-prod to my stomach. Similarly, all throughout the camp the drowsy, exhausted crews expressed surprise and alarm at being taken so quickly. I looked at my captor and the two near him: corsairs of a sort, it seemed. Each wore a simple harness and wore a net of woven weeds at their sides. Their hair was slicked back, and their muscular bodies glistened with seawater in the moonlight. Without speaking, they rustled us together and drove us like cattle into a sea cave at the far end of the beach.

This brutally executed capture was carried out with lightning speed. My companions and I had no time to collect ourselves. I don't know how they felt about being shoved inside this aquatic prison, but as for me, I was shivering all over. With whom were we dealing? Surely with some new breed of pirates, exploiting the sea after their own fashion.

I looked back at Risu, tears streaming down her face now and the last words I heard her utter were these:

"Sorry. I am so sorry."

Then everything went dark.

# Chapter 29

All was darkness. Such utter darkness that my eyes were unable to catch a single one of those hazy gleams that drift through even the blackest nights. From listening to his mutterings, I could tell that Paratiritis was in a state of heavy panic, being deprived of those gracious points of light by which he derived his living. With no stars to gaze at, he sank into a deep depression and sat, motionless, in one corner of the cell, apparently in a trance from which we were unable to arouse him.

We stayed mostly silent for what seemed like an hour but in all likelihood was a matter of minutes. I could hear more of the scholar's mumbled mutterings, the mariner's low hacking cough and the soldier's occasional expletives as he tried to ascertain the dimensions of our prison cell. Then our eyes were suddenly spirited away from utter darkness into blinding light. Our room lit up all at once, filled with a luminescent matter so intense that I first couldn't stand the brightness of it, its sudden glare and whiteness. After involuntarily closing my eyes, I reopened them and saw that this luminous force came from a frosted half-globe curving out from the cabin's ceiling.

"Finally! It's light enough to see!" Encanto exclaimed, dagger ready in hand, staying on the defensive.

"Yes," I replied, then ventured the opposite view. "But as for our situation, we're still in the dark."

This sudden illumination of our cabin enabled me to examine its tiniest details. It contained only a table and five stools. Its invisible door must have been magically obfuscated against divination. Not a sound reached our ears. Everything seemed dead inside this watery prison, but the globe of light hadn't suddenly illuminated without good reason. Consequently, I hoped that someone would soon make an appearance. If you want to consign people to oblivion, you don't light up their dungeons.

We had reason, naturally, to wonder whether similar fates had befallen the other ships which had left the harbour with us. Paratiritis was deeply quiet in his corner of the cell, examining some parchments which I presumed he had the foresight to save from the ship. When I looked up to speak with him, he shook his head and handed them over to me, explaining that he had found them in this very room. They proved to be a brief account of one of our competitors who had found a vast underground temple nearby and, on exploring it, had succumbed to the rapture of the deep - a madness brought on by diving too fast and too deep.

We began to hypothesise on his findings in between readings sections of it aloud to each other, but before we had a chance to fully converse on the meaning and understanding of this find, unlocking noises became audible, a door opened, and two beings appeared.

# Chapter 30

This pair were clearly merfolk akin to Lacrimanta. Though they walked upright on two very human-like legs, their upper torsos were unencumbered by clothing except for a simple leather harness and their skin tinged with iridescent blues and greens. Gill slits adorned their squat, muscular necks, just visible but certainly marking them out as non-human if the hue of their skin wasn't a clue.

They led us down a short corridor of dark, cold, natural stone lit sparsely with luminous blue lightstones until we reached a heavy circular door. One of the beings waved something in front of it and it opened like an eyelid; we were ushered into the darkness beyond. When our eyes had adjusted, I began to take stock of our surroundings and ascertain a means of egress; I could tell that Encanto was doing the same. We stood at the end of a well-appointed long table in a facsimile of a state room, so similar in taste and style to those adorning the mansions of Signici that we were forced to consider that it had been furnished in precisely this manner either for our benefit or - more ominously - as a summation of everything our unknown captor knew about us. I did not like being placed at such a relative disadvantage in this respect and made my opinions known to the others.

More than anything else, I observed the slow, deliberate movements of our captors and wondered who they served, how we might overcome them and what their weaknesses might be. Each was slim in form beneath their voluminous robes and their heads bald and blueish. Their eyes were wide and attentive, their weapons short knives of bone and coral at easy reach on their waists. Neither spoke even when I asked them a question, but seemed to understand what was said and therefore possessed a comprehension of our language and an intelligence at least equal to ours. They bade us by gesture to sit at the table and for the first time we realised we were being fed.

"Interesting!" Encanto's voice echoed in the emptiness of this unearthly hall. "What might they feed us, do you think? Seaweed, no doubt. Perhaps a nice tuna sandwich?"

"Bread seems unlikely!" Giuseppe said. Overlaid with silver dish covers, various platters had been neatly positioned on the azure blue tablecloth, and we sat down to eat. Had it not been for the subdued blueish light flooding over us, I would have thought we were in the dining room of the Hotel Barissima in Lateen. However, I feel compelled to mention that bread and wine were totally absent. The water was fresh and clear, but it was still water—which wasn't what Encanto had in mind. Among the foods we were served, I was able to identify various daintily dressed fish; but I couldn't make up my mind about certain otherwise excellent dishes. There was an abiding tang of salt to many of them - unsurprisingly, given their origin - and a sliminess which seemed to pervade many specimens of fish. These were overcome in part by a manner of different sauces presented in separate, smaller dishes, which we tried eagerly. I paused to give a though as to what the chef Paolo might think of this feast. The abundance of the depths was open before us on the table, but nowhere was their evidence of any of it being cooked - fire presumably being anathema to a cuisine exclusively and extensively sourced from the ocean depths.

Our appetites appeased, we felt an urgent need for sleep. My two companions lay down on the cabin's carpeting and were soon deep in slumber. As for me, I gave in less readily to this intense need for slumber. Too many thoughts had piled up in my mind, too many insoluble questions had arisen, too many images were keeping my eyelids open! Where were we? Intense nightmares besieged me. In these mysterious marine sanctuaries, I envisioned hosts of unknown animals and plants, and this latest setback, so soon after our rescue and discovery of the island... not to mention Risu's absence... my imagination eventually melted into hazy drowsiness, and I soon fell into an uneasy repose.

I tried to fight off this drowsiness. It was impossible. My breathing grew weaker. I felt a mortal chill freeze my dull, nearly paralyzed limbs. Like little domes of lead, my lids fell over my eyes. I couldn't raise them. A morbid sleep, full of hallucinations, seized my whole being. Then the visions disappeared and left me in utter oblivion.

I have no idea how long this slumber lasted; but it must have been a good while, since we were completely over our exhaustion. I was the first one to wake up. My companions weren't yet stirring and still lay in their corners like inanimate objects. I had barely gotten up from my passably hard mattress when I felt my mind clear, my brain suddenly alert. So, I began a careful re-examination of our quarters. Nothing had changed in its interior arrangements. Taking advantage of our slumber, the steward had cleared the table, thus depriving us of any possible weapons with which to defend or liberate ourselves. I sincerely hoped that Encanto had been sufficiently possessed of forethought to conceal some of the cutlery about him during our repast, but I fear he had been too busy opening and closing the tureens in wide-eyed wonder. Consequently, nothing indicated any forthcoming improvement in our situation, and I seriously wondered if we were doomed to spend the rest of our lives in this cell.

When the steward next entered the room, there was a flurry of activity as the soldier seized the opportunity before him. The silver platter dropped to the floor as the steward made a belated attempt to rescue her little coral knife, but too late - Encanto had his burly arm secure around her slender neck.

"Cease this foolishness at once and you will not be harmed."

It was clearly our unknown host who had just spoken, but from where we could not tell. At his words Encanto stood up quickly. Nearly strangled, the steward staggered out at a signal from her superior; but such was the royal authority, not one gesture gave away the resentment that this servant must have felt toward the soldier. In silence we waited for the outcome of this scene; Giuseppe, in spite of himself, seemed almost fascinated. I was stunned. Arms crossed, framed in the doorway, our captor studied us with great care. Was he reluctant to speak further? Did he regret those words he had just pronounced? After a few moments of silence, which none of us would have dreamed of interrupting: "Guests," he said in a calm, penetrating voice, "I speak the tongues of Ilforza, Rivancia and Diviro with equal fluency. Even the ancient script of Arsenia, which you call The Smoking Ruin, is not unknown to me. Hence, I could have answered you earlier, but first I wanted to make your acquaintance and then think things over. Your four versions of the same narrative, perfectly consistent by and large, established your personal identities for me. I now know that providence has placed in my presence Giuseppe, mariner of Ilforza, Paratiritis of lofty Montazzura and Encanto, a soldier born and bred in Lateen whose own brother lingers in a cell nearby." Encanto looked up at this, his eyes wide in surprise. "As for our fourth guest, it is not fate who has delivered you to me but the constructs of your own narrative. I bowed in agreement. The king hadn't put a question to me, so no answer was called for. He expressed himself with perfect ease and without a trace of an accent. His phrasing was clear, his words well chosen, his facility in elocution remarkable.

He went on with the conversation as follows: "No doubt you've felt that I waited rather too long before paying you this visit. After discovering the sum of your identities, I wanted to weigh carefully what policy to pursue toward you. I had great difficulty deciding. Some extremely convenient circumstances have brought you into my presence, I who have made of myself and my people a purpose of remaining unseen by the prying eyes of humanity. It is too convenient to claim that your coming has disrupted my whole existence." I detected a controlled irritation in these words. But there was a perfectly natural reply to these charges, and I made it.

"Your Majesty," I said, "you're surely unaware of the discussions that have taken place in Lateen, Perigee and beyond with your island as the subject. You don't realise that various vessels that have all been searching in earnest for the reputed fortune of your realm and how these questions and quests have aroused public passions on the coast of Ilforza and beyond. I'll spare you the innumerable hypotheses with which we've tried to explain this inexplicable phenomenon, whose secret was yours alone. For our part, we sought only to return your daughter to you, but..."

"And so you have." I looked perplexed at this statement. "So you understand," the king went on, "that I have no right to treat you as my enemy." He paused, as if this announcement in itself was so magnanimous that I should prostrate myself before him in humility at his mercy. I did not. "It took me a good while to decide," the king went on. "I am obliged to grant you hospitality. Were we to part company with you, I'd have no personal interest in ever seeing you again. I could put you all on a ship back to your sea-girted home and even ensure that you had no memory of me or my people. I must admit, that had occurred to me, as both something that I am capable of and would be within my rights as monarch. It is a tactic I have often employed before. Something about the discovery of Farozaina is different this time, though, a ripple in the current that affects even the most distant shore. I wonder if you have even the slightest idea of what that might be?" His eyes narrowed and fixated on me in a way which made me fidget. Wracking my addled memory for what that might be, I tried to recall every legend of this place I had unearthed and committed to paper and performance, but my mind raced too fast to comprehend which element might have been the pebble that caused that ripple.

"I confess that I do not." I replied. "Perhaps you might enlighten me?" I was eager to find out what that might be, gain whatever leverage I could over him. I used to be a master of manipulating narrative. Why did those skills seem to fail me now?

"Playwright," the king replied swiftly, "Your notions of civilization, based on exploitation and competition, are anathema to me and mine." As he raised his voice, a flash of anger and scorn lit up in those royal eyes, and I glimpsed a fearsome past in his life. "When our ancestors fled from disaster in that eastern homeland that still plagues us both with pillage and piracy, yours scattered to the lands and ours found paradise waiting on Farozaina. Generations have since passed, but rather more for your kin than mine. We have learned many more secrets beyond those we carried with us from those desolate plains in the old lands and will not hesitate to use them to deal with anything which we perceive as a threat to our way of life or our very existence."

I realised that what he was saying, effectively, was that no human could call him to account for his actions, nor any concept of divinity as we understood them. Only his conscience - if he had one - or whatever ancient laws by which this society might be governed and which he was bound to follow by virtue of his being their ruler might serve as a check on his behaviour. These thoughts swiftly crossed my mind while this strange individual fell silent, like someone completely self-absorbed. I regarded him with a mixture of fear and fascination. On observing him in detail, I noticed that despite the power imbalance between us, he was regarding me in the same fashion. Two scenarios occurred to me; that he had no more idea of the origin or trajectory of that pebble which had disturbed the placidity of his home waters and was unused to the unknown; that because of that he was treading carefully to avoid further disturbances which might further disturb those waters.

"One last question," I said, just as this inexplicable being seemed ready to withdraw.

"Ask it, playwright."

"By what name am I to call you?" "Well," he replied, "to you, I am His Hadal Majesty, the King Under the Sea, ruler of the Spires of Joy and the Chasm of Sorrow - the heights and depths of Hadala - and the island of Farozaina."

I decided to make an honest inquiry of our royal host. Between mouthfuls of seaweed bread, I asked him what had become of my beloved companion Risu, suspecting the worst sort of news imaginable for in my heart I knew that tragedy was in the air. He stared at me intently and let his bone fork clutter to the platter before him. Wiping his mouth, he spoke these words:

"You are in love with her."

I was about to answer, but he cut in.

"No need to acknowledge. I can see your love and concern writ plainly upon your brow. This is an interesting development, but not entirely unplanned for. You see, playwright, the woman you know as Risu the weather witch, who has watched every step of your travels and whose intelligence, beauty and good humour have lured you here as my catch of the day, is my own daughter, sister to the mermaid Lacrimanta whose discovery set your whole journey in motion."

I sat, stunned at this news, and struggled to formulate any intelligible response in the moment. Our host took this opportunity to take his leave and left me in the banqueting hall, shivering and alone with my thoughts.

# Chapter 31

The next morning - if it was morning, it being impossible to tell in our undersea prison - we awoke groggy again as if we had barely slept. There was fresh water laid out to wash with and some green concoction which evidently was to serve as refreshment. Encanto glanced at the carafe which contained it and decided even the appearance of it disagreed with him.

We sat for a while in an awkward silence punctuated only by the occasional cough. I had not shared the king's declaration about Risu; I could still hardly believe it myself, did not want to imagine how much it might make sense given everything that had happened.

Paratiritis stood and was about to speak when the door opened, and two guards stood outside the cell. "The king would speak with you now. Come."

Encanto looked poised to attack; I could see his muscles tense beneath his smock. I shook my head, and he stood down, looking at me in an appearance of understanding. Truth is, I had no idea what was about to happen or how we would escape from our surroundings, let alone leave the island without a ship. I considered dealing or pleading with the king to still be the best opportunity, but secretly I still longed for the counsel of Risu and her advice. This left me finally pondering recent events as we were led down the dark, damp corridor and cursing myself for not sharing the king's words with Paratiritis, who would surely have given me a lengthy explanation and have offered strategies forward. As I looked over at him, though, I noticed that he did not appear to be lost in thought - his usual expression when he was not elucidating upon some subject of fascination. His brow still furrowed, his arms still crossed beneath the folds of his robes, but there was something different about his eyes. A vacancy, of sorts. Something inside him had already given up. I remembered some of the first words he spoke to me, back at my apartment in Lateen: *I may drown on this voyage.* When I looked forward again, we were being bidden to enter a shallow pool beneath the rock face in front of us.

We swam for some distance, goaded on by the spears of our silent captors. When we had met with the king previously, we had not undertaken any such journey and I began to worry. Had something changed that we were unaware of? Had the king's mood toward us changed as the tides and currents do? Was this to be our end, a final act of doomed heroes? The water above us grew lighter - just enough for us to make out a vertical shaft above us which beckoned us with the promise of the air we were beginning to lack.

Encanto was first to emerge, taking in large gulps of air even as his keen sense of danger took in the scene around him and steeled himself ready to strike. We had emerged into a small pool in front of a much larger one which covered almost all of the floor of the cavern; we could not ascertain its depths without diverting our eyes too long from the rest of the room. Around us were terraces of crumbling grey stone and pure white marble, arranged in rows. On each of these rows there sat more of the merpeople that resembled their king and his daughters - no tails this time, but gills and barbels and scales of glistening cerulean hues. The king himself sat before us on a throne of brilliant rainbow coral. To his left and right were Lacrimanta and Risu, their normal countenances reversed. Upon Lacrimanta's usually mournful and fearful brow there rested a smile of jubilation, excitement even. And instead of the enigmatic smile I had come to expect from my lover's face, there was a downcast expression which spoke of sorrow and loss. When I met her eyes, she winced and gazed away.

It was then I spotted who sat at Lacrimanta's side and realised just how much trouble we could be in, the extent to which we had been duped. Chiaroscuro, the black and white patterns on her robes entrancing with their spirals and swirls, lifted a goblet and nodded at our arrival as the murmur of the crowd fell silent. Behind her, sword at the ready, sat Matthias. Encanto's features contorted into a reddened rage, and it was all we could do to restrain him physically from rushing forward to climb the balustrade toward his brother.

"Traitor! Turncoat! What have you done, brother, that you would sit and sup wine with these creatures while we languor in torment, trapped behind prison walls?" In shock, he tugged a locket from his neck and threw it to the ground in an emphatic gesture. "I renounce you! You are no kin of mine!"

This performance, I was surprised to see, drew a round of muted applause from the assembled throng. I looked over at the tanned mariner

Giuseppe, who was clearly now scared out of his wits and out of his depth. Paratiritis gazed back at me and tilted his head, peering with a look that managed to portray both quizzical and enlightened. "He has seen Risu." I thought. "And is thinking about what that means. He hasn't met Chiaroscuro before…"

The king stood; the voices and echo alike in the chamber descended to nothing, leaving only the sounds of the water cascading down the cavern walls and the stillness of the ocean pool behind us.

"Your journey here has been fraught with many hardships. Hardships we have set in your way and which, unlike some of your fellow competitors, you have overcome. It is natural, perhaps, given our observations of your cultures and your reactions to the dangers you have faced so far, that it comes down to this. My guest here" - he turned and nodded to Chiaroscuro, who offered a perfunctory head bow - "has certain investments in a champion. You stand before me with freedom on your lips, but I offer you more. We offer these tests to those of you on the surface who we consider may be worthy of rewards, and to my people who wish to see how mankind deals with certain kinds of obstacles. Now it is between you and Matthias. The victor, should there be one, will receive our blessings and our knowledge, should you continue to prove worthy."

Whilst we struggled to comprehend the meaning of this speech, two great swordfish jumped clear out of the water and came crashing down, turning over in the air as they did so and flashing their silvery skin in a spectacle of pure exhibitionism.

"Your steeds await." Matthias and Encanto looked at each other in a dangerous mix of drive, revenge and pure horror at the idea, just as a group of large seahorses bobbed to the surface, each with what looked like a harness. Three of Matthias's guildmates stood with him and the mer-captains behind us pointed spears in our direction and goaded us over towards our mounts. Waves of giddy desperation came over me, along with a strange sensation; I realised that I actually *wanted* to partake in this unnecessary melee, to please the crowd, to stand victorious and win the praises of the king and his kind. I could see similar expressions on Giuseppe - who was not trying to fight it, and on Paratiritis who most certainly was.

Matthias and Encanto each mounted a swordfish - not without some considerable assistance - and we managed to get our feet in the seahorse stirrups and secure a one-handed grip which left us still able to wield daggers and clubs. We must have looked ridiculous and were I not in the throes of some preternatural aura I am sure I would have felt so. The king raised to his lips a great hollowed-out narwhal horn and from it emerged a long, low note which reverberated around the arena and signalled the start of our duel.

***

We charged the opposition together, swords raised, as much as our meagre mastery of our marine mounts would allow. The swordfish being much faster, Encanto and Matthias clashed first -

138

Encanto's mount making a failed attempt to impale Matthias's which resulted in a long, shallow scratch along the left flank. Matthias circled round for another pass and the two fish began a deadly duel with their appendages which delighted the crowd.

We closed on the Sarabande, tentatively testing their defences, while making occasional frantic glances over to the 'main event' which was creating a great deal of splashing in the large pool. Matthias and Encanto were close enough now to be daggers drawn but could only get in one or two slashes with each pass of their mounts. The Sarabande, by contrast, made no attempt to attack us beyond defending themselves as excellently and admirably as you would expect from an expert free company. Our endurance began gradually to fade and Paratiritis was first to remark on something we had been taking for granted.

"It appears that our opponents do not actually want to win. Should they desire, they could overwhelm us enough to get past our line and assist their guildmaster against our companion Encanto, but they seem reluctant to do so. I wonder if we should call their bluff and manoeuvre ourselves in an attempt to apparently allow such an opportunity?" I'd noted something myself about our opponents: while they were good, I had expected them to be a lot better. Were they waiting for us to exhaust ourselves? Holding back, waiting for a signal? Why did they not seem as affected by the aura as we were?

Before we could answer our questions, a large gasp from the crowd caused me to turn my head.

Encanto's mount had leaped out of the water through the air and, as we watched in awe and terror, twisted in mid-flight and dived headlong at Matthias, spearing him through the chest. The crowd stood as one and began to cheer. The Sarabande raised their hands in surrender before they had laid even a blow on us, but Matthias was clearly not going to survive without help. Encanto was frantically trying to stop his fish from thrashing around and make the wound worse, but by the time he had done so, there was blood pooling and swirling in the water and Matthias fell off his fish, trying desperately to swim to the edge of the pool with what could easily be his last breath. With a valiant effort, Encanto managed to pick him up and carry him on the back of his mount until they reached the edge, where he lay his brother down and leant over him with concern. Whether there were now tears in his eyes or whether it was merely ocean spray was difficult to discern.

"Well done, brother." Matthias spoke with a thin rattle of a voice, blood seeping from the corner of his mouth. "I knew you would prove the victor."

Chiaroscuro made to stand, but with one glance from the king, she sat again, her expression unreadable even without her custom mask.

"It would appear, esteemed guest, that your champion has lost and that I have won. The knowledge you seek shall not be granted."

There is, somewhere in the depths of Diora University, a well-thumbed book in which have been stitched numerous sketches of various facial expressions, as reference for students of the dramatic arts. Chiaroscuro's changing face at this point contained enough material for a whole new volume: a dawning of downcast rage, mere moments of melancholy regret, a quick-change to quintessential delight and a finale of gloating triumph.

"And what, O King, makes you think that Matthias was my champion as well as my guild's?" She stood now, towering over the king who still sat in the throne on the terrace beneath her, her long shadow twisted in the flickering blue lights of the drowned arena. "I nominated my champion long ago, before this" - she brushed her hand in front of her dismissively - "barbaric mockery of combat was ever announced. My champion is - and always was - the young playwright whose knowledge of your realm is unparalleled in Lateen, who still stands before you. My battlefield is no mere arena constructed for the pleasure of the crowd, but the reams of texts by which we become acquainted with others and reckon their worth; by the exploratory magics of divination and obscuration both; this is the Balance of Twilight. Our wager is not done so easily."

The rage that fell upon the king's face was mighty, but he was compelled to silence by the sudden burst of staccato laughter which preceded Matthias's booming voice.

"Yet, you *have* lost, Chiaroscuro. Do you think I chose my most able combatants for this contest? Do you think the rest of the company lies idle in Lateen, supping sweet wine at the Sybella? No, they have marched upon your headquarters and taken residence, aided by those turncoats of twilight who would want to see your reign as guildhead at an end. Even now, we control your coffers and peruse your papers. You are undone!"

Now her face was a mask of rage and grief not yet captured in any theatre. In a mass of twisted strands of robe and ribbons, she ran, unhindered, for the doorway behind her, in a last attempt to salvage what might be left of her precious guild.

Of the remaining faces among us, mine showed the most surprise. Later, when I had the chance to analyse all the information and fit the stories together, it was obvious - but then so much is when one has the advantage of hindsight. With the addition of foresight, so much might have been avoided and yet...and yet what lay before us now was uncertain. We stood, exhausted and half-drowned, before an enraged king when the primary outlet for that rage had just made exit: stage left.

The king stood, the room again fell silent. Would he pardon us? Let us free? Allow us to rest?

"The show must go on."

No, he would not.

# Chapter 32

A great rumbling interrupted our momentary respite as the arena floor began at first to buckle and then rip open revealing a great chasm, spewing rubble in all directions, and filling the water nearby with a cloud of thick, dark dust which did not at first disperse.

"Behold" boomed the king. "A new test for you all! ...Bid welcome...to my pet... the giant kelp, animated and made to do my will!"

"This is getting quite frankly ridiculous!" swore Encanto, puffing through his breathing spore. "A malevolent giant kelp, whoever heard of such a thing? I swear, you couldn't make this stuff up! What will he have us do next, jump over sharks?"

Paratiritis shot him a quizzical glance and was about to reply when, from the central crater of the arena grew a monstrous sight; a twisted mass of weeds and fronds, writhing and seething with malevolent vitality, brimming with ugly new life. Even as the tendril-like fronds pushed their way through the water toward us, the central stalk thrust upward until the top brushed against the cavern roof. There were gasps and applause from the watching crowd, all 'oohs' and 'aahs' at this new marvel the king had commanded for their entertainment.

I launched myself away from the rock against which I had been resting and swam over to Encanto and Paratiritis, who were both as shocked and exhausted as I. Encanto, ever the man of action, was all ready for another round despite his wounds snaking red streamers of blood about his bicep. He had already begun to hack away at some of the more adventurous serpentine fronds the hulking plant had lashed out with, tingling with luminous venom. Paratiritis looked deep in thought, which would be no help at all. Whilst I had acknowledged there was a time and place for contemplative meditation (I had decided it was 'whilst sobering up between lavish parties'), that time was clearly not during a deathmatch against malevolent toxic flora. I laid a hand on his shoulder to rouse him from his reverie just as he was struck twice in quick succession: first by a sudden inspiration and secondly by a whipping vine which had erupted from the ocean floor nearby, wrapping itself around his exposed legs. The unexpected assault knocked him clean to the floor and he was dragged away from us inexorably toward that central, gaping maw, crowned by a mass of ochre-olive tentacles that quivered in the water like a nest of snakes. Encanto darted forward for a few quick slashes, but again the water slowed both his movement and the impact of his sword, and his efforts were to no avail. We both readied knives in place of other weapons and thrust forward to end off the fiendish fronds and free the young stargazer from a fickle fate. Then came his voice, a choked torrent of hurried commands.

"Rip the plant up! Dive into the chasm and tear up its roots, it's the only way! I've seen this work before, it was…" Just as he uttered these last words and the daring Encanto moved to immediately comply, the kelp raised him high into the water and then, with a great roaring wail which sapped the energy from our limbs, swung him down violently and dashed his head against the jagged rocks on the seabed. The stargazer crumbled into a heap and was immediately still, broken and discarded alike by the creature as a bored child throws away an unwanted toy. The tentacle-seaweed which had held him unfurled and flicked through the still waters in a moment of triumph.

The crowd was awestruck, the king jubilant. I stood stock still, unable to comprehend the sudden death of one who I had come to call a friend, who had shared memories and meals alike. Out of the corner of my eye, I spotted Encanto moving in closer, trying to find an angle of attack and the best approach to fulfil the fated scholar's last words by reaching the roots of the quivering, ululating bulk in the midst of the tangled morass of swirling strands of seaweed.

Then one voice - one voice alone, clear as the bells of the Duomo Capadomus - sounded above the others.

"Enough! Father, that is enough, I beg of you…"

Risu catapulted herself over the balcony, moments ahead of Captain Mauvid's belated attempt to prevent her. She swam swiftly over to me and whispered words into my ear, which made precious little sense even as she urged me to believe her.

"It's your idea! Only you can defeat the kelp, you created it! Oh, please remember!"

I was about to reply that I had done no such thing, but a lurking horror at the back of my mind held me back. Something was definitely not right about this, like a nightmare made flesh. But what could Risu possibly mean, and – more importantly – what could I do? "But Encanto…" I stuttered. What of Paratiritis's idea, the one he had died telling us? Was he to be believed?

"The kelp is a distraction. My father has probed your mind, gathered your thoughts and made them manifest! His magic has sifted through your memories and extracted them for this purpose, making you forget things. Confront my father, not the kelp! I will make everything clear to you in time, dear, I swear it, but you must act now or Encanto will be as lost to you as poor Paratiritis!

I looked deep into her eyes, this mistress of misdirection whom I now realised I still loved. I looked beyond them, to her soul, and saw not the deceptions and lies she had peppered her stories with since first we met. I met the calm within that storm and saw only truth, love, loyalty and my own reflection in the deep swirling pools of her eyes. There was nothing else left.

I resolved to act as directed and think about it if and when I had time, though truth be told my only alternative was to join Encanto in an ineffectual attempt to uproot the mass of thick vegetation which even now still grew unchecked from the gaping abyss in the arena floor. Encanto had made some progress and even now several tendrils were twitching, severed from their parent by his long daggers and heroic strength. He was further wounded and heavily fatigued though and hacking away at a frond which had snaked its way around his neck, ready to tighten its grip and strangle the last life from his lungs. If anyone was going to act now to save him, it had to be Risu or myself – and she had made it clear for some unfathomable reason that it had to be me.

Whilst the king was distracted by the sudden defection of his wayward daughter and issuing commands to his soldiery, I manoeuvred my way along the low wall at the arena's edge toward the stand where he stood. Looking around for more help from Risu, I saw she was engaged now in her own struggle against Mauvid, each dancing daggers around each other. Not only that, there was another struggle inside her – against her own father and sister. It was at that juncture I realised what a momentous decision she had just made and what the consequences would be, the sacrifice she made for our survival. She had been as much a pawn as we had – albeit a smiling, willing one at first – in the game her father had set in motion. I do not think I had ever loved her as much as I did in that moment and resolved to make good my chances to see her plan through.

# Chapter 33

I would here normally describe the manner in which I finally brought low the King Under the Sea - how I first overcame several of his personal guard by flashing blade and dashing deed - and how I won the heart of his daughter. But this is no knightly romance and I have no armour to shine. This is pure theatre, and the manner of endings are different. The deed was done with a dagger to the heart while he was caught off guard by the sudden scream from his other daughter Lacrimanta who had brought nothing but grief and heartache. She had chosen that moment to escape her fate, having decided that doom was soon to be upon them all. I already had the heart of his other daughter, who knelt by my side as we listened to the dying words of the prostrate king. Mine had been hers since we first met.

"Passed...test...all this...yours...rule...wisely..."

As he lay there, my memories - those he had stolen from me with powerful manipulations of revelation and obfuscation which masked even my knowledge of their theft - came flooding back to me like a tidal wave. Each scene we performed, on stage and sea alike, returned at once to me. He had used my theatrical performances, riffs and nuances on the Farozaina stories, to build an adventure for us all - as Chiaroscuro knew he would - one in which I was the protagonist both unwilling and unknown. All done to test our reactions to situations, our responses to stimuli, observe our fates. And at what cost!? In an attempt at revealing this information, at enlightenment, he had used secrecy, illusion, deception, those very tools of obfuscation which are their equals and opposites. If you have to use lies to serve truth, what then does that say of the service? Only that both are required - an amalgam of day and night both - a balance of twilight, if you will, from dusk till dawn.

As the king finally passed away, we looked up from the water to the ceiling of the cave and beyond - high above the Spires of Joy to the surface, to the island of Farozaina and beyond to the bay.

# Chapter 34

We had little idea as to what the funeral rites might be for our Montazzuri friend. We decided that his pragmaticism and practicality would be foremost and that he would consider his body of work more important than his physical body. We bound his notes and the sketchings of the night sky I made to accompany them: Giuseppe and Encanto promised they would arrange for them to be shipped to his academy once they were safely back in Lateen.

Risu sang a lament at the solemn but brief service. I think this is the only occasion on which grief suited her. Tears streaked unchecked down our faces as we stood over his body.

As for Encanto and Giuseppe, they got their dreams of riches. In return for their efforts and their silence, they became the first humans to ever leave the shores of Farozaina. Safe in their hold was a fortune in pearls and priceless art, sublime corals and chests of coin. They looked at me and I looked back. At that moment they knew - though I think they knew before - that we were not going to accompany them. Giuseppe shook my hand firmly, his head bobbing and teeth glinting as he smiled. Encanto even ventured a hug, but looked embarrassed about it afterwards and stood back, arms folded.

We swore oaths of lifelong loyalty and marked the occasion with a gift of bracelets, fashioned by Risu from delicately woven silverweed and depicted a mermaid clasping a single shimmering pearl as if it were a mirror. They promised to keep in touch. I laughed and doubted it were possible, though with the array of magical tools at my disposal I supposed it were possible I could contact them if I so wished. Matthias, likewise, had all of Chiaroscuro's research at his disposal and seemed inclined to share it if he could. Whatever had passed between the brothers seemed over now, an aura of calm on that tempestuous ocean of sibling rivalry.

Of Chiaroscuro and Lacrimanta, we heard no more. Were they to lay plans against us, to harbour revenge in their shadow-laced hearts, it would not come to fruition soon. Time would tell.

Meanwhile, I had a kingdom to rule and new magics to discover. It would also be some time before I truly mastered either. Who can fathom the soundless depths? Risu had no doubt I would - that, she said, was the reason she believed I had been chosen for this role, by manifest destiny or by deeds well done.

Now I sit here on the throne of Hadala, Risu is by my side, laughing and smiling: my constant companion through trials and tribulations, through love, loyalty, and devotion until the end of our days.

## THE END

Milton Keynes UK
Ingram Content Group UK Ltd.
UKHW040746030624
443647UK00001B/3

9 781786 958785